# GOING ROGUE

## SAS ROGUE UNIT - BOOK 1

## LOUISE ROSE-INNES

*For all those who have served.*

# 1

Grant Kerridge pulled his Suzuki GSX-R sports bike up on its rear stand so the back wheel was off the ground, then bent down to inspect the chain. He grunted in disgust. After his last cross-country expedition, it was filthy with road dust and splattered with mud. He pulled on his latex gloves, reached for the rag he kept on the workbench for just such occasions and set it down next to the chain cleaner and the circular brush. Time to get stuck in and give this baby a clean.

His favorite classic rock album was playing in the background, louder than his neighbors would have liked, but he needed the noise to drown out the voices in his head.

*"TAKE COVER!" yelled Joe, his signaling expert and best mate, when the unit first came under fire. "Contact to the north."*

*Grant threw himself into a meagre clump of bushes to the side of the mountain path which offered no cover whatsoever, especially not against flying bullets, but it was enough to get him* out of the worst of the onslaught. Joe wasn't so lucky. He took a bullet in the leg and went down with a yell.

Rick, who was closest to him, tried to help, but he was gunned down within seconds. Grant watched in horror as he performed a macabre dance of death while he took several rounds in the back. Then he fell face down onto the Afghan dust and didn't move again.

"Hang on, I'm coming." Grant twisted his head to work out from which direction the shots were coming from.

"No, stay there," Joe shouted. He was lying on his back in the middle of the path, totally exposed, firing his automatic weapon up towards the high ground, a grim expression of determination on his face. His leg was bleeding profusely, forming a dark red puddle beneath him on the dry dirt. It needed a tourniquet or he'd bleed out.

Grant ignored his friend's warning and crouching low, ran to assist.

"Cover me!" he yelled to the two remaining members of his unit who had scattered into the brush beside the path. He heard Chris open fire a few meters behind him. They were sitting ducks in this valley, with militants firing down on their position, but his overriding priority was to get Joe off the path and out of the line of fire.

Vance, the medic of the team, appeared on the opposite side of the path. Together, they grabbed Joe by the arms and pulled him off the path into the undergrowth, hoping to find shelter beneath a small rocky outcrop.

Vance took off his belt and tied it around Joe's thigh, stemming the flow of blood.

"Hang in there mate, we're going to get you out of here."

Joe nodded, his face pale. "Rick?"

Grant shook his head. "Nah, he's gone, mate."

The haunted expression in Joe's face said it all. Rick had been in the regiment for eight years, give or take, and in their unit for the last five. They were as close as teammates could be.

Vance didn't comment. They knew from experience they had to focus on the present situation if they wanted to get out of there alive. There would be time to grieve later.

"Where's Sayed?" Grant looked around for their translator, the Afghan local who'd led them this far into the field on their reconnaissance mission to contact local populations in an effort to regain control of the region.

"Pissed off as soon as the shooting started," came Vance's reply. "Bastard gave us up."

Grant looked around for an escape route. Nothing sprung to mind. Above them, the hills were dotted with militants, all with rifles trained down into the valley. He thought about traversing the opposite side, but knew they'd be picked off as soon as they moved.

"Call for backup," he ordered Joe, who shrugged out of his rucksack and got the patrol radio out.

"Zero-Alpha, this is Three-Two-Charlie. We have a man down and require assistance. Over."

A tinny voice replied, "Three-Two-Charlie, we read you. The Afghan army is closest, and we've sent them your signal. ETA twenty minutes. Over."

Christ, in twenty minutes they'd all be dead.

"Can you send a chopper? Over."

"Will do. Get yourselves to the rendezvous point. ETA one hour. Over."

Even worse. He glanced at Vance who gave a little shake of his head. That would be too late. They needed extracting now but it was not possible. They were on their own.

From the south came more gunfire. For a split-second Grant thought it might be friendly. Maybe the Afghan troops had arrived early, but he soon realized his mistake. It was another militant group approaching from the south, pinning them in. He watched as they slid down the mountain like an army of little ants with guns blazing.

They were ambushed in the valley with no way out.

"We're going to have to fight our way out," said Chris, joining them under the rocky outcrop. "We'll have to split up."

Grant knew his explosives expert was right. Normally, they stayed together as a group, but in this instance, they'd be a bigger target and easier to hit by the snipers hidden up in the hills. The only problem was he had Joe who was injured and couldn't walk. He'd have to carry him out which would slow them down.

"Leave me," rasped Joe, who'd read the situation and knew the deal.

"Shut up." Grant refused to even entertain the thought. "You and I are going together or not at all." He looked at Chris and Vance. "You guys go, we'll be right behind you."

They looked like they might refuse, then Joe said, "There's no point in us all dying out here. Bugger off, you lot. We'll meet you at the RV point."

Chris wavered, then made up his mind, saluted and disappeared back the way they'd come, keeping low and sticking to the sparse cover of the shrubs alongside the path.

"Let's at least try to get him to some decent cover." Vance poked his head out from behind the outcrop and stared up at the hills. He could see smoke from rifle fire and several shadows moving amongst the trees.

Supporting Joe beneath each arm, they got him to his feet, but before he could move, a bullet hit him in the stomach and then another in the chest. He went down, a dead weight between them.

Grant let out a strangled yell. "Joe!"

Vance shuffled back under the outcrop, but Grant dropped to his knees, cradling Joe's head in his hands. His friend gargled something and Grant bent forwards, trying to hear.

*"What's that?" The emotion threatened to choke him. He knew there was no saving his friend now. He was going to die out here in this war-torn country, far away from home.*

*"Tell Lilly I love her," he rasped, before his head went limp and fell back onto Grant's knee.*

*Vance patted him on the shoulder. "We've got to get out of here, man. Leave him."*

*Grant nodded. They'd send a team in later to extract the bodies. Right now, they had to concentrate on getting themselves to the rendezvous point for the helicopter extraction.*

*"Good luck," he said to Vance, who nodded and snuck out from the other side of the outcrop and slithered like a snake on his belly up the hill to deeper cover.*

*Grant took one last look at Joe, then melted into the shadows at the base of the hills.*

A LOUD METALLIC knock bought him back to his senses. "Hey, Grant. You there?"

Grant got to his feet, recognizing the voice. It was Pat, Joe's father, a man he'd got to know well over the last ten years since he'd met Joe during selection. Pat was an army man himself, more specifically, a retired army commander of the paratroop regiment. A tough old bastard, Pat weathered most storms – like the passing of his wife from cancer four years ago and his forced retirement from the army – with quiet dignity and control. The only time Grant had ever seen him cry was at his son's funeral four months ago.

"Yeah, hang on." He pressed a button and the garage door rolled up with a harsh metallic scrape that made his ears curl.

"Needs some oil," grumbled the commander, ducking his head and coming inside.

Grant took off a latex glove and shook his hand. "Pat, what brings you out this way?"

Since he was no longer part of the SAS 22 Regiment, Grant had moved to a quieter part of the Herefordshire countryside. There was a lake nearby that contained some decent trout and he had a fishing boat that he took out occasionally.

"Thought I'd come and see how you were doing," said the commander, his eagle eyes taking in the gloves, the bike and the assortment of cleaning materials on the floor. "You giving her an overhaul?"

"Just cleaning the chains. She got a bit dusty this last trip."

Pat perched on an upturned crate and studied Grant for a long moment. "So, how are you doing, son?"

Joe's death had been a turning point for Grant. After the chopper had taken him and Vance to Fort Bastion – Chris hadn't made it out – and they'd been debriefed, he'd decided he'd had enough. He'd lost half his unit in that ambush and had no one to blame but himself. Vance had gone AWOL that very night, while Grant had flown back to the United Kingdom with Joe, Rick and Chris's bodies, which had been retrieved by the supporting Afghan forces later that day.

Grant didn't look him in the eye. "You know..."

"Yeah, unfortunately I do."

Grant pulled on his gloves again and picked up the cleaning fluid. He aimed the nozzle at the chain, spun the tire and sprayed the overlapping portions of the rings on the lower rung for a full revolution. Then he took the brush and spun the wheel again, allowing the chain to pass through the bristles with a low hiss.

"I think about it all the time," he murmured once the wheel had stopped turning. "I can't get it out of my head."

"You've got to let it go," said Pat leaning forward. "It wasn't your fault. It's a goddamn war out there. Joe knew the risks, so did the others. It's pointless blaming yourself."

"I should have seen it coming. It was a bloody ambush. I was the one who led them to their deaths." He turned back to his bike, picked up the rag and wiped off the excess liquid.

Pat was silent for a moment, then he said, "How are you keeping busy?"

Grant shrugged. "I take this baby out, I go fishing, you know, the usual stuff."

"Bored?"

Grant glanced up. "Out of my mind."

Pat got up off the crate. "Let's go inside. I could use a brew and I've got a proposition for you."


"Do you remember Joe's girlfriend, Lilly?" They sat opposite each other on two wooden benches either side of the oak table in Grant's kitchen sipping coffee. After years in the field with no milk to be had, they both drank it black and strong.

"Lilly? Oh, you mean Lillian? Yeah, I remember her."

Grant had a vague recollection of Joe's girlfriend, a slender, waif-like girl with short, dark hair and thick glasses. He'd always thought her a bit of a nerd. They'd been together forever, but she didn't socialize much with Joe's special forces buddies. When Joe was on leave he made himself scarce, spending most of his time with Lilly, and Grant always assumed, her friends. "She worked with computers or some such, didn't she?"

"She's a smart girl. She works for GCHQ now."

Grant was impressed. GCHQ was the British equivalent of the American NSA, an intelligence organization aimed at defending the country from cyber threats, supporting law enforcement as well as the armed forces. In the Regiment, they'd often used GCHQ's data on ops ranging from satellite images to foreign intel. But why was Pat telling him all this?

"That's great, Pat, but what's this got to do with me?" He wasn't one to beat around the bush. He saw the corners of Pat's mouth turn up, and the commander gave a little nod.

"I'll get to the point. She's gone missing, Grant, kidnapped while in Kabul on a project for the British government."

Grant stared at him, a knot growing in the pit of his stomach.

"Kidnapped by who?" he said slowly.

"We suspect the Taliban."

"We?" He narrowed his eyes. He knew the retired commander still had his fingers in a lot of government pies. It kept him busy, and it kept him from thinking too much about his wife and now his son.

"I'm an unofficial consultant to the Home Office on this. What I'm telling you now can't go any further, you understand?"

"Of course."

He nodded, a flicker of sadness passed over his face, and Grant realized just how worried he was.

"Lilly was on loan to the Afghan government." He leaned across the table, his voice deep and low. "She helped them upgrade their military software, a move that would go a long way to removing the Taliban from the opium-rich Helmand Province."

"So, they grabbed her to prevent it from going online." Grant finished for him.

"Oh, it's online," Pat confirmed, a note of pride in his voice. "She was en route to the American base along with a small group of reporters, to fly back to the U.K. when the Taliban struck. The soldiers accompanying them were shot and killed and she was taken along with the reporters."

"Why now?" asked Grant, getting straight to the point. "Isn't it too late if the system is already online?"

Pat looked grave. "She is one of three people who have the top-secret codes they need to dismantle the system. The other two are Afghan military operators whose identities are unknown. She was the easier target." Pat reached for his coffee and took a slow sip. Grant waited until he was done. "With those codes they can render the entire system useless. All her work will have been for nothing."

Grant was silent, studying his best friend's father across the table. His rugged, tanned face was pinched and the fine lines next to his eyes were deeper and more pronounced. This meant a lot to him – she meant a lot to him – he could tell. The knot in his stomach began to expand, gnawing at him from the inside.

"Why are you telling me this?" he asked, dreading the answer.

There was a pause, then the commander said, "I want to go and get her, Grant. And I need your help to do it."

"Isn't this a job for the Regiment?" Grant leaned back in his chair, arms crossed in front of his chest. "That's what they do, and you know as well as I do, that nobody does it better."

Pat put his mug down with more force than was necessary. "The Home Office won't sanction it. The Taliban and the top Afghan powerbroker have just finished two days of landmark talks in Moscow and they don't want to rock the boat. As you know, we've withdrawn all our troops from the area, and the Americans are talking about doing the same. An insurgency now would destroy everything."

"Surely the Taliban knocked that for a six when they kidnapped her?"

"They're claiming they weren't responsible, but it's bullshit. We have satellite images of the attack and intel of activity at a known Taliban stronghold where the hostages were brought late last night."

"Any visuals of the hostages?" he asked, wondering what condition they were in.

"We're sending in drones to pinpoint their exact location."

Grant gave him a hard look. "Why bother with the intel when they're not going to send in the special forces?"

"I didn't say they weren't going to send anyone in, I just said it wouldn't be sanctioned." He met Grant's gaze. "That's where you come in."

Grant didn't respond. A million thoughts were flying through his mind, none of them good.

Pat continued, "I know you have contacts, guys who've left the regiment who are dying for some action. I figure we need a team of four, that should do it, plus me, of course, to feed you with the intel. We can hitch a ride on a military plane to Bagram tomorrow at oh six hundred hours."

Grant exhaled slowly, trying not to let the panic rise within him. He could see this meant a lot to Pat. Lilly was the only link he had left to his son and the old man wanted to do something. He got that. But he was barking up the wrong tree coming here.

"You know I can't do this, Pat. I'd love to help, but after

what happened before…to Joe and the others… I don't think I'm the right man for the job."

Pat studied him for a long moment, then said, "I'm asking you to put your own situation aside, Grant, and do this for me. For Lilly. She's like a daughter to me. I can't leave her there to rot. God knows what those bastards are doing to her."

"I wish I could, really, but I'd be a liability. There are better men for the job."

"Listen to me," Pat said, standing up. "You were the leader of the best troop in the best regiment in the best army in the world. There is no one better for the job."

"I was, Pat. Past tense. Besides, I'm not battle ready. I wouldn't be able to tab 20Ks without stopping."

"Please…" Pat wasn't buying. Grant was still in superb physical shape. Sure, he'd taken a knock but he still ran every morning, worked out in his spare room which was filled with gym equipment. Some habits were harder to break than others and he enjoyed feeling fit. It was one of the few things that motivated him these days and Pat knew that.

"Come on, Grant. I need you on this. It's the only chance she's got."

Grant bit his lip. Shit. The last thing he needed was to relive the trauma of that last op. Going back to Afghanistan would bring it all back, the pain, the loss, the guilt… It was insane to even consider it.

"What about kit?" he asked.

"All will be provided at the base. It's been cleared, unofficially, of course."

It seemed the commander had thought of everything.

"Christ, Pat. I don't know if I can."

Then, he said the words that would change everything. "It's what Joe would have wanted."

Grant sighed. It was true. Joe's last words came back to haunt him.

Tell Lilly I love her.

Well, he hadn't done that yet. She hadn't been around to tell. Maybe it was time he did.

He nodded slowly. "Okay, old man, you win. I'm in."

## 2

Lilly awoke from an exhausted sleep and cringed as the aches and pains from yesterday penetrated her fragile consciousness. They'd walked for nearly eight hours over rocky terrain, through the night, until they'd arrived at this place. She looked around at the filthy room with nothing in it other than a soiled mattress, a bucket, and a wooden chair with a missing leg that wouldn't support anybody's weight, and grimaced.

She knew she was in a town or village of some sort because she'd heard the sound of children crying and dogs barking late last night when they'd arrived, and she'd smelled the aroma of cooking food, not that they'd been given anything to eat or drink since their capture. Her stomach rumbled as if pressing home the point.

She'd been separated from the other hostages, much to her dismay, and locked in here for the remainder of the night. At least having the English journalists with her had made the nightmare seem more bearable, and she was able to talk to them to stave off the growing terror. One of them had even spoken Pashto and had translated for the rest of the group so they'd known what was going on.

This way!

Keep going!

Don't fall behind!

Basic commands, but it was so much better knowing what their captors were shouting at them than being left to wonder.

Now, she had no way of communicating with her captors unless they spoke English, which was highly doubtful. After four months of living in Kabul and integrating with the local community, especially the women, she knew the Taliban tribal factions were made up of men from rural communities acting on orders from tribal leaders. Some of them had no choice, they did it in order to survive, whilst others were searching for a cause, trying to make sense of the war-torn chaos.

She also knew why she'd been taken. The military software system. They wanted access to it and the only way they could do that was via the codes she had set up. No one else knew the codes other than the two Afghan software developers on her team, Nabi and Anwar, who she'd trained and whose job descriptions read Office Administrator so no one looking at the facility's employment records would suspect them. A copy of the codes was also stored in the Commander of the Afghan Army's safe in an undisclosed location.

She was the weakest link.

The small window at the top of the wall let in a hard shaft of light, the beams of which picked up the dust hovering in the room. It was almost pretty. Lilly shuffled across the floor until she was under the light, then turned her face up to it, wishing she hadn't lost her glasses on the trudge through the hills. Judging by the temperature and the position of the sun in the sky, it was late morning. She'd been in this stinking room for over twelve hours. Someone would come for her soon.

She shivered as she thought about what lay ahead. Torture, for sure, as they tried to extricate the codes from her. She could play dumb, pretend she didn't know anything about the codes, but she suspected they'd done their homework and knew she was the one who'd upgraded the software. That would only work for so long.

She swallowed repeatedly trying to generate some saliva. Her mouth was parched. What little water she'd had on her had been left in the vehicle along with her handbag (containing her British passport) and suitcase. Lack of food and water made her weak and she shuffled back to the dirty mattress. Perhaps, they were going to leave her here to die of starvation and dehydration? Maybe their main focus had been the journalists, and she had been in the wrong place at the wrong time? Under the circumstances, that would be the preferable option.

No such luck. There was a scratching outside the door and a young woman, her head and face covered, entered carrying a tray. She placed it at the foot of the mattress and with a little bow, retraced her steps towards the door.

"Wait." Lilly scrambled to her feet.

The woman paused, her eyes aimed at the ground like she was afraid to look up.

"Thank you." Lilly gave a little bow like she'd seen the local women do.

The woman nodded then exited the room. Once again, the key turned in the lock.

Sighing, she went back to the mattress and sat down. So much for trying to establish contact. On the bright side, the tray had food and drink on it. It was only a flat bread along with a jug of water but Lilly fell on it like it was a gourmet meal. She'd finished eating when the key turned again and the door creaked open. This time a man in traditional dress and a turban stood in the entrance. He beckoned for her to follow him.

THE DRIVE NORTH took another full day but as far as Lilly was concerned while she was in transit, there was little chance of them having a go at her. They would leave that task to a Taliban leader, someone with the authority to coerce the information out of her and the know-how with which to do it.

She had a bag over her head for most of the journey, but she kept listening in the hopes of identifying where she was going. It didn't do any good. Apart from the spluttering and ticking over of the old Ford engine, she couldn't determine anything distinctive. The men spoke Pashto which meant she couldn't understand a word, and apart from fastening her seat belt for her, she was completely ignored. There was no sign of the other hostages. With a heavy heart, she wondered what had become of them. Were they to be ransomed off? She'd heard kidnapping was big business in the Middle East these days. Governments and indeed wealthy families, maybe even media companies, would pay large amounts in ransom to have their citizens, employees, and loved ones back. Money that could be used to purchase weapons and bribe officials.

Tears sprung to her eyes as she thought about her own circumstances. There was no one back home to pay her ransom. Her father had disappeared when she was a toddler and her mother had died in a horrific pile-up on the M4 motorway several years ago. Since then, she'd only ever had Joe.

Her heart twisted painfully, her loss still raw despite it being four months since his death. Darling Joe... her rock... the person she'd clung to, who had always been there for her through thick and thin.

Oh, why did you have to die?

With Joe in the 22nd Special Air Service Regiment she'd known the day might come when he left on an op and didn't return. She'd steeled herself against that inevitability, but even so, she'd been so unprepared to lose him, so unprepared to live her life without him. They'd been together for over ten years, ever since he'd signed up for the Regiment and made it through selection. She'd been there for him every step of the way, as he had for her. Tears stung her eyes under the foul-smelling hessian bag. Joe would have come to rescue her, she knew that without a doubt, but now there was no one.

Eventually, the car stopped and she heard doors opening and footsteps on the gravel ground. Cold air flooded in. Her body tensed, waiting for someone to unbuckle her and take her to her holding place, the place where she would be tortured.

There was no chance of rescue. She didn't kid herself that she was important enough. She was a civilian, not some high-powered politician or powerbroker upon whose shoulders a fragile peace agreement rested. She was expendable, a computer nerd who'd done some work for the government. In addition to that, she'd be almost impossible to find. They'd moved her from the village to the mountains, judging by the extreme freshness of the air and the fact that

the car had been travelling steadily uphill ever since they'd
set off.

She had the military codes, this was true, but once the
Afghans heard of her kidnapping they would put the backup plan (that she'd devised) into action and reconfigure
the codes. Nabi and Anwar knew how, she'd trained them
well.

The thought gave her a small comfort. At least the
Taliban would need her alive and (relatively) unharmed to
get into the system and override the codes. She was the only
other person who could. No, she mustn't give up now. There
was still hope.

After she was unbuckled and dragged from the vehicle,
the bag was removed from her head. The sunlight was
blinding and she blinked furiously, eyes watering while they
tried to adjust.

Rough hands half-pulled, half-dragged her towards
what appeared to be a jagged mountain ridge, but then as
they rounded a rocky outcrop she saw a dark slit that
marked the cave entrance. Looking around, her heart sank,
she was literally in the middle of nowhere. There wasn't a
house or a farm in sight. The view, however, was breathtak-
ing, and on any other day she would probably have enjoyed
it. From her vantage point, she could see for miles across the
fertile valley with a twinkling azure river carving through it.
The undulating hillside was blanketed in luminous green
fur upon which shadows danced whenever the wispy clouds
obscured the sun. There wasn't time to admire it in more
detail as she was pushed inside the cave and made to sit
with her back against the cold rock wall while a young man,
who couldn't have been older than about nineteen, chained
her ankles to two wrought-iron rings embedded into the
solid ground.

Crude, but effective, she thought grimly. With these shackles on she wasn't going anywhere fast.

"Please, can I have some water?" she asked, extending her arm, but he moved out of her reach and shrugged, like he couldn't understand.

"Water," she begged, making a drinking motion with her right hand.

He gave a little nod and disappeared back the way they'd come.

Lilly didn't have to wait long before an older man with a long beard and flowing robes entered the cave carrying a flask of water. By the way he carried himself, she reckoned he was the one in charge. He sat down opposite her, crossed-legged, and set the water down on the ground just out of arm's reach.

"Salaam," he said politely, although his face remained impassive. "I hope you are not too uncomfortable."

Was he kidding?

She needed the bathroom, a long drink and a shower, preferably in that order. And to be released from these iron shackles might be a good start.

"I'm okay," she replied, keeping her eyes down in a submissive gesture like she'd seen the women at work do when talking to their male superiors. She'd be damned if she was going to beg him to go to the toilet, if there even was one around here. At least in the village there'd been a bucket in her room. Here, in this cave, there was nothing.

He nodded in approval. "Do you know why you have been bought here?" His English was heavily accented but grammatically correct and she got the impression he was well educated, definitely the one giving the orders.

She shook her head. "For ransom?"

It was, she hoped, a convincing shot in the dark. The last

thing she wanted to do was let on she knew about the military software system and the codes. If she could make them think they had the wrong person, she might have a fighting chance of getting out of here alive.

He studied her, his dark eyes narrowed and filled with suspicion.

"What is your name?" he barked. He wanted to confirm she was who they thought she was.

"Jo Burke," she said, using Joe's name and surname. It was the first thing that popped into her head and in some weird way gave her strength. Joe wouldn't have backed down in this situation. He'd have fought until the bitter end, and then when that had come, he would have gone out fighting. A lump formed in her throat as she thought about him. Hopefully, the Taliban leader would think it was fear.

He sucked in air over his teeth. "I believe you are lying to me. Your name is Lillian Devereux and you work for the Afghan government."

She shook her head, disappointment welling up inside. They knew. Still, she stuck to her guns. "No, that is not my name. I am Jo Burke and I am a journalist with The Guardian newspaper in London." She knew Felicity, one of the other hostages, worked for the Guardian. Hopefully, the correlation would give her story credibility.

The man slammed his fist down onto the hard ground. "Liar. You are Lillian Devereux. Here is your picture." He threw a laminated card at her feet and with dismay she recognized it as her work keycard which she'd used every day for the last four months to get inside the secure government building. How on earth had they got hold of it? They must have bought someone off or had a man on the inside.

She hung her head. Faced with the damning evidence,

she couldn't very well keep on lying. Her little charade was over.

"Now, I ask again. Do you know why you are here?"

Keeping her lips pressed firmly together, she shook her head. She might be Lillian Devereux, but she wasn't going to give him the luxury of answering his questions. If he wanted her to speak, he'd have to force the words out of her.

"I will tell you why. You are here because you have something we want. Something that is very valuable to us. I think you know what that is?"

Go to hell.

She kept her mouth shut and her eyes cast down. God, that glass of water looked inviting. She fantasized about gulping down the cool, thirst-quenching liquid and began to salivate.

"You can have it, I brought it for you." His voice was back to being calm and conversational. "Once you tell me what I need to know."

Want to know, she thought savagely. You don't need to know anything. You want to know so you can stop the Afghan army doing their job and kicking you out of Helmand Province. The opium-rich region had been terrorized by the Taliban for decades. The local farming communities were divided, with half working the poppy fields and paying tariffs to the ruthless war lords, and the other half living in fear trying, mostly unsuccessfully, to run legitimate businesses.

She clamped her mouth shut even harder.

After a long moment, the Taliban leader got up and sighed. "I'm sorry you feel that way. You are making things very hard on yourself."

And he picked up the water flask and left the cave.

.   .   .

THE SAME THING happened later that night. The bearded man came again, this time bringing a plate of food and another flask of water, as well as some blankets and a lantern. It was freezing in the cave now that the sun had set. In particular, an icy-cold draft swept through the room like a fan was on, but when she peered in that direction, all she saw was shadows. Lilly gazed longingly at the blanket but didn't utter a word. As she'd done earlier in the afternoon, she kept her eyes lowered and refused to speak.

In frustration, the man left again, taking everything with him but the lantern. She still hadn't gone to the toilet or eaten or drunk anything. Her last meal had been earlier that morning when the robed woman had brought her the tray in the village. The food and drink she could last without for a while longer, but she really needed to relieve herself. She knew what their plan was, now. They were going to rely on her modesty to beg them to take her to a toilet and they'd refuse, unless she offered up the information. The same went for the water and the food. Nothing, until she cooperated. Well, it was better than torture, she supposed. Although, how long before their patience ran out?

First things first, she had to empty her bladder. Her modesty was not something she was particularly attached to, and with the cave empty, now was her chance. She maneuvered herself in a semi-circle until she was as far away from her previous position as she could get. Her ankles twisted painfully in their metal bindings, but she didn't want to have to sleep in a wet spot, so she pushed it as far as she could, then pulled her trousers down and her underwear to the side and relaxed.

That was so much better. Luckily, the cave had a gentle slant and the liquid ran away from her. She felt a smidgeon of satisfaction knowing they couldn't use that against her anymore. She resumed her position, hugging herself to try and generate some heat. Thank goodness for the lantern, it offered a glimmer of light in the darkness. Without it she might have succumbed to the fear that surrounded her heart and threatened to crush it at any given moment. The cold was her biggest worry. If they didn't give her a blanket or light a fire, there was a very real possibility she might die of hypothermia during the night.

The man didn't come back again, obviously deciding to let her stew overnight. In the morning, when the cold, hunger and thirst had taken its toll, he'd try again.

It must have been about two hours after sunset when Lilly heard a ruckus outside. She'd been trying to doze off, to sleep through the worst of the cold and also because she was mentally and physically exhausted, when a shout brought her to her senses. Fully awake, she huddled against the wall wondering if this was part of their plan. Had they come to frighten her, or worse, to harm her in some way in an attempt to get her to cooperate?

She gasped as she heard a deafening volley of automatic fire. It wasn't continuous, but rather several short bursts followed by shouting and sporadic blasts of return fire. Then she couldn't determine what was going on as a cacophony of firepower erupted meters from the entrance to the cave. The Taliban youth ran in waving his weapon above his head and shouting something to her in Pashto. She couldn't understand him, but she knew it wasn't good, so she curled up in a ball and tried to make herself as small a target as possible.

There was more yelling and shooting, and then a monster of a man ran into the cave. He looked like something out of a futuristic horror movie, silhouetted against the light, with helmet-mounted goggles covering half his face and an enormous gun aimed at the terrified teenager. Before she had a chance to shout out, the invader pulled the trigger and cut the youth down in two short bursts from his automatic weapon.

Then he turned to her.

## 3

"Lillian Devereux?" the monster asked.

She scarcely heard him, her gaze was riveted on the bullet-ridden body of the youth lying at her feet. Blood oozed from his forehead. He'd been so young.

"Lillian! Is that you?"

English. He was speaking English. It filtered through her stunned mind that he must be here for her.

"Yes," she whispered, then realized he couldn't hear her.

"Yes." More strongly.

"Good. I'm going to get you out of here." He bent down to inspect her shackles, then pulled a lethal-looking combat knife out of a leather sheath attached to his belt. Her eyes widened as she recognized it. Joe had an identical one.

"You're special forces," she gasped as the man pried the lock loose, lifted the shackles and released her.

He gave a curt nod and reached down to haul her to her feet. "Come with me."

She stumbled, her ankles bruised and unused to supporting her weight, but his grip was firm and he steadied her. "Okay?"

After a moment, she nodded.

He led her towards the dark slit that was the cave exit. She couldn't wait to get outside. They almost made it too, before all hell broke loose.

"Get back!" he barked, as gunfire rained down from above. The noise was deafening. Lilly stumbled backwards into the cave and out of the line of fire. There was a crackle and she heard a tinny voice radiate from his ear-piece. He was communicating with the other members of his team.

He put a finger to his ear. "Okay, you guys get the hostages clear. I'll bring out Lilly."

Something about the way he said her name rang a bell, but she couldn't quite place it. Was this one of Joe's SAS teammates? Had they met before? She tried to get a better look at him, but it was dark in the cave and the night-vision scope covered half of his face, the other half in shadow.

"No go. I'm not having history repeat itself. Get those hostages to safety, that's an order. Over." He was shouting now, tension in his voice. This wasn't good.

"We're going to retreat into the cave," he told her, grabbing her wrist and pulling her towards the back of the cave. "Or look for another way out."

"I felt a cold draught from that direction." She pointed to a dark recess to the right of where she'd been bound. "I think there might be a tunnel there or something."

He moved to where she was pointing and lifted the night-vision goggles from his eyes. "You're right. There is a narrow tunnel here with cold air blowing through it. It's a pretty strong breeze. I think it could be another way out."

"Can we fit through it?" she asked doubtfully. It was very narrow, about four feet wide by three feet tall.

"There won't be much wriggle room, and I'll have to leave my bergen behind," he patted the heavy rucksack on his back, "but it's our best option. The insurgents are covering the front exit and there are more coming down from the hills, so we can't get out that way without support."

Which you sent away, she added silently.

"I'm going to booby trap the cave entrance," he explained. "So stand right back. Hopefully, this will buy us enough time to get away."

"What if we can't get through the tunnel?" Fear made her voice come out higher pitched than normal. "We won't be able to come back this way after you blow it up."

He gave her a wry grin. "No, but on the bright side, the enemy won't be able to get in, either. It's the only option we've got."

Great. So he was going to blow up the only exit and take his chances in the narrow tunnel. She watched as he reached into his rucksack and took out several squares of explosive wrapped in masking tape. He placed them strategically around the cave entrance and then laid a thin wire across it, several inches from the ground, which he connected to the explosives. After inserting several plugs and grips, he stood back to admire his handiwork.

"That should do the trick."

Lilly yelped as a bullet hit the rock a meter from where she was standing and sediment sprayed into her face. She only just managed to close her eyes in time. Her savior released a deafening volley of automatic fire through the entrance. It was so close and so loud that Lilly covered her ears. Halting, he turned to her. "Come on, let's get out of here. I'll go first. Stay behind me."

He switched on the light mounted to his helmet and eased himself into the tunnel. His massive shoulders took some maneuvering, but then he was in. She watched as he leopard-crawled along for a few meters. Her eyes were drawn to his khaki-clad butt, which was impressive in itself, but she wasn't in a position to enjoy it. The dark tunnel ahead filled her with dread. They were actually doing this.

"Looks safe enough," he called, stopping to peer ahead into the darkness. The breeze is strong. I think we'll be okay." A few seconds later he disappeared from view.

Well, if he can fit, so can I.

Dark, enclosed spaces weren't her favorite thing. Taking a deep breath, she ducked down and scrambled in after him. The ground beneath her fingers was cold and crumbly, and it had a metallic smell that would have been sharp and pungent had it not been diluted by the breeze. They progressed slowly, inch by inch for about twenty meters, him in front of her and her focusing solely on his wriggling butt. It was taut and firm and helped keep the panic at bay. Eventually, the passage widened and they crawled into a small, rounded alcove where they could both sit side by side.

The soldier was wiping sweat from his face. "We can rest for five minutes."

Thankfully, Lilly pulled her legs through into the alcove and sat next to him, her back against the wall. The stiff breeze made the confined space more bearable, and she wanted to believe the hilltop and freedom were only a short distance away.

"You okay?" the soldier asked her. The light attached to his helmet was still on so his features were a dark haze. She didn't dare ask him to turn it off because it would be pitch black in the tunnel without it and that would probably send her over the edge. His voice was familiar, she tried to place it, but couldn't.

"Yes, I–I think so."

"Good." He pulled out his compass and studied it for a

minute. "We've been going steadily west and in an upwards trajectory, so I'd say it won't be long until we reach the outside. Fifteen, twenty minutes max. Do you think you can handle that?"

What choice did she have?

"Yeah."

It couldn't come fast enough for her. The tunnel was dark and claustrophobic, and she couldn't stop thinking about what would happen if it narrowed to a point where they couldn't get through. What then?

A muffled blast made her jump and sent a puff of dust up the narrow tunnel. She glanced at the solider in alarm, only to see a spread of white teeth. He was grinning. "I'm guessing they tried to enter the cave."

How could he be so calm? She felt the rising panic in her chest. Their only entrance was now blocked off permanently. There was no going back.

He must have read it in her eyes, because the teeth vanished and he laid a firm, calloused hand on her arm. "Stay calm, Lilly, and keep breathing normally. We're almost out."

"Have we met?" She wondered again at the familiarity with which he said her name.

She couldn't see his face but knew he was looking right at her. Hers, on the other hand, would be illuminated by his headlight.

"Yes, I'm Grant Kerridge, Joe's friend from the Regiment. I'm sorry I haven't been in touch before now, but you left so soon after he... he passed away. Joe gave me a message for you. He said to tell you that he loves you."

## 4

Okay, so he wouldn't win any prizes for his delivery, but at least he'd said it. He'd told her.

The look on her face was one of complete astonishment and she opened her mouth to speak, but he held up a hand effectively cutting her off. Now was not the time.

"Come on, let's move on. We can talk when we're outside and safe."

She shut her mouth and nodded.

Turning his back on her, he crawled further up the tunnel. The angle was noticeably steeper now, and the breeze was stronger than before. It blew the hair back off his face, a sensation he relished, for it told him they were on the right track. Escape, evasion and survival, that's what he was trained for, and during his operational days, he'd crawled through way worse than this to stay alive – they all had.

He thought grimly of Jamie, Cole, Alex and Pat, his makeshift unit, who would be guiding the freed hostages through the thick, impenetrable forests that covered the valley to the rendezvous point where a waiting chopper would transport them to freedom. They were a good bunch of guys, he'd served with them all at one time or another during his special forces career. They were effective, able, and deadly. Even though the Taliban fighters would be close on their tail, he was confident they'd get the hostages out in time.

Peering ahead into the tunnel, Grant estimated they had at least twenty to thirty meters to go before they broke ground. It was doable, as long as the enemy weren't waiting for them at the other end.

Grant knew from experience that things hardly ever went according to plan, this op was a classic case in point. You could prepare down to the finest detail, but inevitably something would happen to fuck it up. The enemy was an unknown force, impossible to control, and that's why you always had to ask yourself what if?

What if there were more insurgents than they'd expected? What if the hostages weren't there? What if one of them was injured? What if the helicopter couldn't make it to the emergency rendezvous point? What if? Well, good thing Grant had plenty of contingency plans.

At the U.S. air base at Bagram, before the Apache helicopter had brought them out here, he'd studied drone footage of these mountains and knew they were crisscrossed with tunnels, the Taliban's favorite hiding place. He was betting on the fact that the enemy below hadn't yet realized they'd left the cave. That would give them several hours to get as far away from here as possible.

It was night time, so there was no light to mark the end of the tunnel, nothing to break the engulfing darkness. The only clue he had was that the air was colder now and made his eyes water. They must be close. He rounded a curve and hit a dead end.

What the...?

He reached out with his hand but all he could feel was cold, hard stone. His heart dropped. No, this couldn't be. He heard Lilly scampering up behind him. "Why have we stopped?"

How could he tell her there was nowhere to go?

Another blast of icy air hit him. It seemed to be coming from above. He glanced up and realized with a start that the tunnel made a ninety degree turn upwards and there was a hole at the top through which he could see the stars.

Brilliant. They'd made it.

He recalled there was a crescent moon tonight, which was perfect because it gave them enough light to see by but wouldn't leave them too exposed. There would be plenty of shadows in which to hide.

The only problem was getting up there. He gauged the distance to be about ten foot. Too high for him to reach, but together they might have a shot.

"We're at the end," he called to Lillian who'd stopped behind him. "There's a hole vertically above us, but it's high and we're going to both have to squeeze in here for me to get you up there."

"Thank God." He heard the relief in her voice.

"Good. I'll get to my feet and then you crawl as far forward as you can, until you feel my legs, then slide up next to me."

"Okay."

He got to his knees, scraping his back against the stone roof of the tunnel. Ignoring the pain, he held onto the walls as he straightened up. It was tight, but he estimated there was just enough room for the two of them. The problem would be getting her into a standing position. His arms scraped the sides, and he forced himself to stand as far back as he could, so that the hard, jagged edges dug into his back.

"Now your turn."

He heard her scramble forwards until he felt her hand on his shin.

"That's it. Come as far forward as you can but watch your back. Now work your way up. It's a tight fit, but we can do it."

"I don't know if I can." Her voice was hollow beneath him and he could hear the stress in it. She was seconds away from panicking. "There isn't enough room."

He pushed his legs back as far as he could.

"Listen, Lilly. The only way we're going to get you out of here is if you climb up my body. You're going to have to use me like a ladder. I can help you, but you've got to get to your feet first. Don't worry about me, push against me if you have to, but stand up."

She shuffled forwards some more. He felt her head bang into his knees, then his thighs and then into his groin. He didn't move in case he put her off. His body, however, was reacting to her closeness, and he fought to keep himself calm. He'd switched his head-lamp off when he'd stood up, so as not to attract any unwanted attention from above, so the glimmer from the unseen crescent moon was their only light source.

She grunted as she turned her face sideways, so it wouldn't be plastered against his stomach and slowly managed to slide onto her knees and then finally onto her feet. She'd filled out a bit since he'd last seen her, which admittedly was almost a decade ago. Her hips dug into his and her breasts pressed against his torso. With every breath, he felt the softness of her chest expand into his.

"Are you sure about this?" she whispered, her face inches from his. He could feel her breath on his lips.

"I'm sure." He kept his tone calm and even. Her hair cascaded round her face and tickled his neck, and despite her hours in captivity, it still smelled faintly of lavender. She tilted her head to glance upwards at the hole, but her nose bumped his.

"Sorry," she whispered, and he sensed her discomfort.

"Let's get you out of here," he whispered. "I'm going to lift you up from the waist as far as I can, then I want you to stand on my shoulders until you can clamber out of the hole."

She nodded, and he felt her nose rub against his again almost like an Eskimo kiss. Their breath mingled in the darkness and he felt so close to her that for a fleeting minute he considered leaning in to let their mouths meet. It wouldn't take much, less than an inch. What would she feel like? Taste like? Would she respond?

In light of what he'd just told her about Joe, probably not. It was a stupid idea, but given the confined space, it was one his mind was having a hard time letting go of.

"I'm ready," she said.

He placed his hands around her waist and lifted her upwards, her body flush against his. Her breasts bounced into his face, so he twisted his head to the side so as not to embarrass her. They were lovely breasts, though, and he resisted the urge to nuzzle them. Then he chastised himself for his primitive response. *Get a grip, soldier*. She was a hostage and his best mate's girl. He needed to stay focused, which meant not reacting like an adolescent schoolboy.

She wasn't as heavy as he'd expected, so he was able to get her high enough so that her hips were level with his shoulders.

"Can you grab onto anything?" He grimaced as his elbows scraped against the hard rock.

She bent her knees and put one on each of his shoulders, stabilizing herself. Her groin was right in his face, but she didn't appear to notice. She wore lightweight cotton trousers and he could feel the lace from her panties right through them. He felt himself stir.

Bloody hell. The sooner he got her out of here the better.

"I can feel a plant or a root or something," she whispered, stretching upwards. Her pelvis tilted so that her crotch was right in his nose.

"Grab it," he muttered. "Quickly."

She managed to hang onto something to give her leverage and pulled herself up until she was treading lightly on his shoulders. He breathed a sigh of relief. Her musky scent had been driving him insane.

A few seconds later, she'd scrambled out.

"How are you going to get out?" She peered back into the darkness.

"Take this." He held up a length of rope. It had been tied around his waist and was easy enough to grab hold of in the confined space once she'd gone.

"Tie it to a tree but keep your head down in case anyone's milling about." The last thing he wanted was for a Taliban sniper to spot her, although they'd be under strict orders to shoot, not kill. They needed her alive for the codes, she was useless to them dead. With him on the other hand, they wouldn't be so particular.

Soon, there would be insurgents all over the hillside searching for them. His team hadn't counted on a rebel army descending from over the ridge, and he still didn't know exactly where they'd come from. They must have been hiding out in the cave network that riddled the mountains.

At least Alex, Cole and Jamie had secured the four other hostages, and had escaped into the forests in the valley below seconds before the attack from above. It had taken him longer to find Lilly, since her captors had separated her from the other hostages, probably to interrogate her in private. She was their prize. The others were collateral, an added bonus to use for ransom.

From what he'd seen, Lilly didn't appear to be injured or harmed in any way, which was one reason why they'd inserted as soon as possible, perhaps to the detriment of a more thorough reconnaissance. It was vitally important she didn't sabotage all her hard work on the military system by hacking into it and giving the Taliban rebels full access. Pat had outlined how important her work was to the Afghan government, and he knew the enemy would stop at nothing to extract those codes from her.

The end of the rope dropped down into the tunnel. She'd done it! He gave it a firm tug, then climbed to freedom using the walls as leverage.

## 5

W ith the cold night air on their faces, they crouched low and ran across the rocky terrain towards the tree line five hundred meters below. Despite it being spring, the temperature had dropped close to zero overnight, and their breath misted up in front of them, particularly Lilly's, which is how Grant noticed she was breathing harder than normal.

"When did you last eat or drink anything?"

"Not for a while," she admitted, doubling over to get her breath back. She was fading fast, her blood sugar dangerously low due to dehydration and lack of food.

"Let's stop here for a moment," he said as soon as they'd reached the cover of the trees. She stopped next to him and wobbled, unsteady on her feet. He put out a hand to stabilize her. "We should be okay here for a moment."

She nodded and leaned back against a tree trunk before sinking down onto her backside. The leafy branches overhead arched down like a green thatched roof providing cover. Now they were in the forested area, it would be a lot harder for the enemy to spot them, if they were even look-ing. The cave collapse would take hours to clear, and the Taliban would assume they were still inside. Grant esti-mated they had until daylight before Lilly's captors realized they'd escaped. Then they'd follow the tunnel and start scouring the hilltops, eventually tracking them into the forest, which was the only logical escape route

He unclipped his water flask from his utility belt and pulled a soft energy bar from his pocket.

"Here," he said, handing them to her.

Wordlessly, she took the flask in one hand, tilted her head back and drank, her eyes, the color of the dark canopy above, not moving from his. Next, she tore open the energy bar and took a greedy bite. Her eyelashes fluttered, breaking contact, as she chewed and swallowed, then she took another bite, and another, until the entire bar was gone.

"Thanks, you're a lifesaver." She crinkled up the wrapper and looked around, unsure of where to put it.

"Give it to me." He held out a hand. "Any rubbish we leave behind will let the Taliban know we were here and which way we went."

There was a short pause, after which she said, "I remember you. You're the leader of Joe's unit. I remember seeing you guys together once or twice in the early days."

Before she'd wrapped his best mate around her little finger and he'd stopped hanging out with his SAS buddies.

He wondered if she was thinking the same thing as him, that they hadn't taken to each other when they'd first met. He'd thought Lilly, or Lillian as she was known back then, was too smart for her own good. Definitely too clever to mix with the likes of them. He recalled how she'd dismissed him with one flat glance as a brute, a tool for violence and not a person she approved of or wanted to associate with, at least not socially. Why she'd stayed with Joe all those years was a mystery.

"Was the leader," he said with a rueful grin. "I left the Regiment after... Well, a couple of months back."

"After Joe died?" She regarded him silently. The whites of her eyes were very clear and bright in the light of the crescent moon.

He nodded.

She looked away. "I heard he wasn't the only one who lost his life that day."

Grant swallowed over the lump in his throat. "I lost most of my team that day," he managed. "And, I was the only one to make it home." Vance, the only other survivor, had gone off the grid. According to rumors, he was living in a rural Afghan village and had converted to Islam.

After a beat, she asked, "Will you tell me what happened? I know the official version and what Pat, Joe's dad told me, but I'd love to know what really happened."

Oh, boy.

Grant looked down at the ground wishing it would swallow him up, but he knew this wasn't a conversation he could avoid.

"The official version isn't far off," he began, waiting for his heartrate that had escalated at her question, to return to normal. "Pat knew about it. He would have given it to you straight."

She laughed softly. "No, he tried to protect me like the M.O.D. did, like everybody did, but I don't want the watered-down version. I want to know the cold hard truth about how Joe died."

Grant studied her as best he could in the dim light.

She'd lost the glasses he remembered her wearing, big, black-rimmed things that did nothing for her looks. Without them, he could see how pretty her eyes were, slanting up at the ends. And her skin was pale and smooth, only marred by the redness of her lips. Those eyes were questioning him now, and those lips were pouting, waiting for answers. He sighed. Personally, he thought the watered-down version was better, for her, anyway. She'd loved Joe, spent ten years of her life with him. Did she really want to taint her memories by the cold, hard truth, as she put it?

"Are you sure?" he asked.

She nodded.

Well, if that's what she wanted...

"We walked into an ambush," he began, staring at a blade of grass growing through the bark at his feet. "Our translator was a Taliban sympathizer and unknown to us, had given away our location." He paused for a moment, the guilt hovering over him, giving him a headache. "I should have seen it coming," he added with a desolate shake of his head.

She didn't speak, just watched him with narrowed eyes.

"The mountain pass was in a valley surrounded by hills on either side. It was a perfect natural trap. Insurgents descended from both sides and opened fire on us. We were completely exposed. We ran for what little cover there was, but Joe wasn't so lucky. He took a bullet in the thigh and went down.

Lily blinked but remained silent. He had no idea what she was thinking. Her expression gave nothing away.

"Rick went to help him and..." He paused as the memory of Rick's body floundering, taking round after round, flickered in front of his vision, burning his eyes.

"And?" she prodded.

"And he was gunned down," he finally got out. "I tried to pull Joe clear, but he took another round in the chest. There was nothing I could do." His voice turned into a rasp, and he exhaled slowly through pursed lips.

It hurt so much to talk about it.

Goddamn it, Joe.

Which was why he didn't. It was easier keeping these visuals buried like some bittersweet home movie hidden at the bottom of a drawer to be viewed and cried over when extremely drunk.

"And Chris?" she wanted to know. He raised an eyebrow. She knew the names of Joe's fallen colleagues, but not his. Perhaps she would have remembered if he'd also died on the mountain pass like he ought to have done.

"Chris was shot by a sniper as he made his way to the rendezvous point."

"So only you and Vance made it out alive?" She made it sound like an accusation. He didn't blame her. For months he'd thought the same thing. How had he made it out in one piece? Was it blind luck? Or was God tormenting him by making him live with the guilt for evermore. Was that his punishment?

"Yeah, the chopper was waiting and transported us out of there back to base."

"And Joe's body, along with the others, was left on the path?" Her voice cracked and he could sense the tears filling her eyes, even though she wasn't looking at him.

"Only temporarily," he said quickly. "They were retrieved later that day when it was safe to return to the region." When the Afghan army, assisted by an airstrike by the British RAF, had taken out as many of the Taliban fighters as they could. The rest had disappeared back into their tunnels to fight another day.

She took a deep breath and cleared her throat. "And you were the one who brought him home?"

Them. He'd brought them home.

He nodded, not trusting himself to speak.

And then he'd buried them.

Come to think of it, he couldn't remember her at the funeral.

As if reading his mind, she said, "I couldn't do it. I couldn't go to the funeral. I paid my respects privately."

It was none of his business. "You don't need to explain."

"But I want to." She paused and fixed her gaze on him like this was important, like she wanted him to understand. "The month before, GCHQ had offered me this position in Kabul, and I jumped at the chance. I thought it was a way to be closer to Joe, and it was a chance to do something to end this awful war."

If she thought one software program could end the decades-long conflict in Afghanistan she wasn't as smart as he'd thought she was.

She continued, "I know it's not the same as being out there fighting, but it was better than sitting at home doing nothing. And if the Afghan government could use it to drive the Taliban out of Helmand Province and restore peace to the people in that region, I would have accomplished something." He couldn't argue with her there.

She hung her head. "I flew out the week after he died. It was easier that way. I had to get away from the memories. Everything at home reminded me of him. I wanted to do something constructive to take my mind off Joe." She scoffed. "Except being out here, seeing where he was based, it made me miss him all the more."

Grant could understand that.

"I'm sorry," he said. "It was my fault we got ambushed. I didn't vet the translator thoroughly enough. It was my job as team leader to double-check all third parties, and I let them down."

Her eyes roamed over his face as if gauging whether he really meant it. Well, he did. More than she would ever know. He lived with the thought that perhaps if he'd been more careful, if he'd scrutinized Sayed more closely, then maybe, just maybe, his friends would still be alive today.

Eventually, she said, "I don't blame you for what happened. You couldn't have foreseen that ambush. Pat told me you'd relied on faulty intelligence. You weren't to know the translator was one of them."

He stared at her through haunted eyes. Pat had divulged a lot more than was necessary, but then she was the type to demand details. He probably hadn't told her anything she didn't already know.

Her gaze hardened. "But, I do blame you for making him join the bloody SAS to start with."

"What?"

"It was you who convinced him it would be a good idea to join a bunch of killers. I know it was." She took an angry breath. "You might work for the government but you're the last resort, the killing force that they bring in when all else fails."

He couldn't deny it. That was exactly what they were. Glorified killers, trained to take out the enemy with extreme prejudice and capable of extreme violence when necessary. And he was proud of it.

But he hadn't coerced his friend. That bit wasn't true.

"Joe wanted to join the 22 SAS," he said slowly. "There is a selection process. We went through it together."

"Yes, but he joined the military to train as an engineer before you convinced him to sign up for the Regiment." Her voice pierced his heart with every word. "If it wasn't for you, Joe would still be alive today."

## 6

It was hard to believe this was the same man as she remembered. Grant Kerridge had been famous in Hereford. From his rippling muscles and a six-pack he didn't mind showing off, to his easy smile and witty banter, he was every woman's wet dream. He was tough too, outperforming most of the others in training exercises, and according to Pat, a natural born leader. She couldn't deny he was good-looking in a rugged, outdoorsy kind of way. Tanned and fit, with a strong jawline and laughing, blue eyes.

Joe had looked up to him, almost hero-worshiped him, a trait that had bothered Lilly to no end in the beginning of their relationship. Joe was bright, very bright, he could figure out how anything worked, take it apart and put it back together again. He would have made a brilliant engineer. But that's not what he wanted. No. He wanted to follow his cocky, self-assured friend into the death squad and join the SAS.

How had she not known it would end this way?

Joe wasn't like Grant and Rick and the others. He was

strong, yeah, and he'd been well-trained, but he was a softie at heart and the kills bothered him. He struggled to process what he'd done. He had nightmares. Once, a few weeks before he'd deployed, she'd woken up to find his hands around her neck. Luckily, he'd come to his senses and realized what he was doing before he'd done her any harm. When she'd suggested he get some help, he'd flatly refused, saying they'd kick him out of the Regiment if he was diagnosed with PTSD, a fact she knew to be true. Personally, she hadn't thought that was such a bad thing, but the unit had become his life, his teammates his family, and of course, Grant, he'd looked up to like an older brother.

Grant bent down in front of her to tie his shoelace. She marveled at his somber face, etched with fatigue and determination. He looked the same, still ruggedly handsome, but the eyes weren't laughing anymore.

"If you've got your strength back, we should probably get moving."

Lilly ached from head to toe, but she gave a curt nod and got to her feet, surprised when Grant held out his hand. "I'm okay, thanks."

Since her little outburst, he'd clammed up and hadn't said another word, preferring to stalk around their resting place, his weapon at the ready, keeping an eye out for the enemy. She too, didn't think it was likely they'd be detected until morning. It was too dark to clear the debris from the cave tonight to see if they were still there, and no reason to believe they wouldn't be. No, she was pretty certain they had at least five- or six-hours head-start to get the hell out of here. Grant's pacing was his way of avoiding talking to her.

She was glad she'd got that off her chest. She did blame him for Joe's death, indirectly, of course. He shouldn't have been in the Regiment to begin with. She allowed herself a small daydream about what might have been. Her and Joe at home, married, a baby on the way, him working at the nearest base as an engineer, building airplanes or weapons, or something else he was passionate about, and her going to work at her computer job, knowing full well that Joe would be there safe and sound when she got home.

Sadly, that's all it was, a dream.

She glared daggers at Grant's back as he led her further into the forest. He seemed to know where they were going, despite the dense trees blocking out the moonlight and making everything look the same. Every few meters, he'd turn to check up on her, to make sure she was still stumbling along behind him.

They didn't speak, the only sound being that of their footsteps, or rather hers, and the small animals she heard scurrying into their burrows as they approached. Grant seemed to glide through the undergrowth, barely making a sound, which was bizarre given his massive bulk and those enormous boots he was wearing. He was easily six foot four or five and almost as wide. When he'd lifted her up in the vertical tunnel, he'd done so effortlessly, as if she weighed nothing more than that blasted rifle he carried with him. Heat stole into her cheeks as she thought of how she'd had to rub against him to get out. He'd been so hard, so firm, and he'd smelled so masculine that it had awakened a longing in her that she hadn't experienced since Joe.

God, she missed his body, missed having his arms wrapped around her at night. But most of all, she missed his smile of delight when he woke up next to her in the morning, like she was a wonderful surprise that he hadn't been expecting. Even after ten years together, he still did it.

Had done it.

Joe was gone. Why couldn't she get her head around that?

They walked on for at least five kilometers, by Lilly's rough calculations. The forest was thinning out and so they began to move sideward, along the contour lines, instead of down into the valley. He wanted to retain their cover.

"Where are we going?" she eventually asked, breaking the stony silence. Her natural curiosity had gotten the better of her.

"There's a cabin about ten klicks... Sorry, I mean ten kilometers ahead."

She knew what a klick was, but she nodded. She didn't ask how he knew about the cabin, she assumed it had been part of their preparations.

Every now and then, he'd speak into his earpiece, but didn't get any reply. He just kept repeating the same thing.

This is Call Sign Two Zero Alpha. Over.

Nothing.

Then twenty minutes later, he'd say the same thing.

"Who are you trying to contact?" It was obvious no one was there.

"My unit," he replied curtly, but gave no further explanation. After a long pause, he added, "They're out of range."

On they trudged, until Lilly felt her legs giving way. She was exhausted and perspiration ran between her breasts and under her arms. She didn't want to know what she smelled like. Her eyes felt like they were filled with dust and grit from the tunnel, but that was probably because she hadn't slept for nearly twenty-four hours. They'd been hiking through this forest for an eternity. The sky was lightening towards the east, shimmering with a soft, electric blue glow that signified they had another hour or two at the most before sunrise.

"I don't think I can go much further," she puffed, after stumbling yet again.

"We're almost there," he said, glancing behind him. "Do you want me to carry you?"

God, no.

But she wasn't sure her legs could hold out much longer. He took the matter out of her hands, and slinging his rifle over his shoulder, he walked back and scooped her up.

She gave a half-hearted cry of protest, but then relaxed against him. She was too exhausted to care. Mustering a protest required energy and she had none left. Not an iota. So she closed her eyes and laid her head against his shoulder as he transported her the last kilometer to the cabin.

With her eyes shut, Lilly felt every little muscle movement as he walked, or rather strode through the forest. His bicep bulged under her head, creating a surprisingly comfortable pillow, and she could feel his pecs moving under her cheek. Not knowing where to put her outer arm, and not wanting to dangle it down making it harder for him to carry her, she folded it on top of her stomach, her hand splayed open against his chest.

Big mistake.

Now with every step she felt his heart beating, firm and steady, as he carried her to safety. He smelled good too, like a man. Like Joe smelled when he got back from a day at the barracks. It had been so long since she'd smelled that manly scent that she inhaled deeply, savoring it. As they gained more ground, her mind grew groggy and before she knew it, she'd lapsed into an exhausted sleep.

## 7

Grant knew the second she fell asleep. Her body went limp and her head relaxed against his arm. He glanced down and for the first time, took a long, hard look at the woman he'd rescued. The stress lines on her forehead and around her eyes were gone, making her appear calm and serene. There was a rosy blush on her cheeks from the exertion, but she also had faint purple shadows underneath her eyes, a testament to the ordeal she'd undergone.

He had to take his hat off to her, she was tough. They'd covered nearly twenty kilometers in the last five hours, not an easy feat in mountainous terrain where the ground was uneven and full of bulging roots and surprising dips, yet she hadn't complained once. Not a single wince or moan, until she'd been about to collapse.

He felt bad for pushing her so hard, but she had really pissed him off with her comment about Joe only joining the Regiment because of him, in addition to which, they needed to get to the security of the cabin before daybreak.

Was it true?

It was so damn long ago he could hardly remember. They'd met at a training camp. Joe was a soldier in the Royal Engineers and Grant had recently returned from a tour in Iraq with the paratroopers. Grant was older than Joe by about five years, but they were both adults and military men to boot, so age didn't mean a thing. They became fast friends. Joe had always been bright, and he was... had been... an asset to their unit. The guy had been a genius with machinery. Anything from their patrol vehicle to a jammed anti-tank weapon, he could take apart and fix.

But had he convinced his mate to sign up? Thinking about it, Grant remembered the moment he'd decided to try out for the Regiment. He'd outgrown the paras. The constant partying and mayhem while off-duty was taking its toll. He didn't like the person he was turning into. To win the respect of his mates, he had to drink more, stay up later, and get up to more shit, and after four years, he was over it.

Then one day, on a training operation in Germany, he'd been in the canteen when the atmosphere changed. It suddenly buzzed with energy like an electric current had been fed thorough the room, and in walked a massive, tattooed man with a barrel chest, wearing a beige beret with a distinctive emblem on it, that of the winged dagger. Grant remembered staring at the man with respect and admiration. The entire canteen had gone quiet, as if the sheer power of this one man had rendered them all speechless. This was a member of the Special Air Service, the British army's most elite fighting force.

As soon as he got back to England, he went straight to his Commanding Officer and applied for selection, the grueling six-month recruitment process for the 22 SAS.

Perhaps his determination had rubbed off on Joe, but one thing he was certain of, was that his mate wouldn't have signed up if he hadn't wanted to. As he recalled, Joe had been as driven as he was. During selection, which was one of the toughest courses in the world, they'd both managed to keep it together and neither had broken. If Joe had wanted out, he would not have made it through the tough physical endurance, the jungle training, the escape and evasion, or the interrogation training. He wouldn't have coped with the hunger and thirst, the intimidation tactics, or the sheer exhaustion they'd experienced for days with no apparent end in sight. No one without a hundred percent commitment would have.

Grant had the utmost respect for anyone willing to put themselves through that grueling selection process. There was no shame in bugging out. Many good men had. Not everyone was cut out to be part of the 22 Regiment. But Joe wasn't one of them.

He grimaced. Whatever Lilly might think about him, she was wrong about that. Sure, he might have talked about it, but Joe had made up his own mind about joining and had been all-in from the get-go.

The cabin was situated in the densest part of the forest, barely visible unless you knew it was there. Abandoned for many years now, it would have at one point been a half-way house for bandits and rebels. Now, given its dilapidated state, it had been left to rot. Cole had rebuilt the front door yesterday morning after the chopper had dropped them off. He'd attached new hinges and repaired the lock so that it could be bolted from the inside. The windows had been boarded up, apart from a tiny slit at the very top, so not only was it fairly dark inside, but no one could enter that way unless they had a rocket propelled grenade - then, he thought wryly, anything was possible.

He kicked the door open and went inside. He knew immediately his mates had been back. There were two fully-stacked bergens in the corner. Thank you, lads. These were definitely going to come in handy since he'd left his rucksack behind in the cave.

He glanced at his watch, badly scratched by the tunnel. It was twenty past five in the morning. By now the rest of his team would have landed at the Bagram air base and the hostages would be enjoying a cold beer on their flight back to England. Mission accomplished. All except his part.

He laid Lilly gently on the floor, then folded up a blanket and placed it under her head. She stirred but didn't wake up.

He smiled when he saw a note in Pat's barely legible scrawl on the table.

Glad you made it out! Left you some supplies. Good luck.

It was unsigned. No clue for the enemy in case they'd found the cabin before Grant had made it back there.

The supplies Pat had mentioned were in the bergens. He began to unpack them. There were rations and water, a first-aid kit, five pounds of Semtex including detonators, stun grenades, hand grenades, blankets, a sleeping bag and a small gas cooker – everything a special forces operative would need to operate behind enemy lines. Unfortunately, but for obvious reasons, they'd taken the radio equipment with them. It wouldn't do to have that falling into the wrong hands.

Grant secured the premises as best he could. He set an early warning system outside using some of the explosives, so if anyone approached the cabin, he'd hear them. Next, he bolted the door from the inside, and only once he was satisfied, did he sit down and eat and drink something.

While he ate, he thought about how quickly he'd mobilized the guys to come out here. None of them had needed much convincing. He'd called Jamie and Cole first. Jamie was at home with his sister and younger brother, both of whom he looked after and who were getting on his nerves. After being kicked out of the Regiment for not following orders, which in reality meant sleeping with their assigned Officer's wife, he'd gone into the family business. He'd taken over the running of his late father's garage but was going stir-crazy without any real action. It was only a matter of time before he got into a bar fight or a pub brawl to break the monotony, he'd told Grant on the phone.

Cole was in a similar position after taking two bullets to the chest in an op that went south. He'd spent a month in hospital and another two rebuilding his strength and going to compulsory therapy sessions during which time he'd been diagnosed with mild PTSD. The SAS wouldn't touch him after that. To say he was upset was an understatement. Cole had always been an adrenalin junkie and a major risk-taker, which was precisely why he made an excellent soldier. PTSD or not, Grant didn't think the guy could get any crazier. One thing he did know for sure was that in a firefight, he wanted Cole on his side.

Alex, who despite his lightness of foot was pushing forty, had opted out of the Regiment voluntarily at the end of his term and was trying to enjoy his retirement, but instead of peaceful evenings on his patio enjoying the sunset, he found himself longing for the excitement and the camaraderie of the unit. When Grant had called about the unofficial op, he'd jumped at the chance.

It was a pity he hadn't managed to get Lilly out of the

cave in time to make the RV, but after what had happened on his last mission, he wasn't about to risk his team getting blown to bits. He'd much rather they get out okay, then live with more deaths on his conscience. He would just have to get Lilly out of Afghanistan alone.

Grant yawned and thought about getting some shut-eye. He'd been awake since the flight to Bagram the previous night and although he'd been through worse, that faint sense of disassociation that came with severe fatigue was setting in. Even as he gazed at Lilly sleeping peacefully on the blanket, her curvaceous form began to swim before his eyes. With a resigned sigh, he lay down next to her and pulled the extra blanket over them both. Within seconds, he was asleep.

"Joe," she moaned in his ear. Grant thought he was dreaming, but then she snaked an arm over his chest and whispered again, more huskily, "Joe."

He lay stock still, unsure whether or not to wake her. He knew by the light shining in through the horizontal slit that it must be about midday. They'd slept for several hours. Tentatively, he put a hand on her shoulder and gave her a little shake.

"Lilly, wake up."

"Uh-uh," she murmured and snuggled into him some more. Her hair tickled his chin and her hand was now stroking his chest.

"Lilly," he said louder, but he had to admit, he was enjoying the gentle onslaught. Her hand caressed his chest and stomach and she nuzzled him gently.

"Lilly, wake up."

"I don't want to," she muttered, draping a leg over his.

He stiffened. What was happening? Was she awake? He

lifted his head and glanced down at her face. Her eyes were closed.

Her leg moved up and down, massaging his thigh. It felt good. She felt good. He brushed a stray hair out of her face and thought how sexy she was with her lips parted and her eyes closed and her body all languid and warm. How come he'd never noticed before? He suddenly saw what Joe had seen in her, and what he'd been blinded to by her superior attitude and fast put-down. Those horrendous glasses hadn't helped either.

But as much as he was enjoying this, he couldn't let her continue. She'd be so embarrassed when she woke up. "Lilly, come on. It's time to wake up."

"Kiss me, Joe," she whispered, sliding her head onto his chest.

Whoa!

He couldn't stop her as she angled her face upwards and found his lips with her own. His pulse accelerated and he knew he ought to put a stop to this. Surely, she wouldn't...

But she did.

Her lips were warm and soft and he found himself responding despite his better judgement. Her arm snaked around his neck and buried up into his hair. He groaned, it felt so good. How long had it been since he'd made love to a woman? Too long. Not since before his last tour, before his world had come crashing down around him.

Her mouth moved against his, probing it open. He let her lead, hesitant to reciprocate in case she woke up and got a fright. Perhaps she'd sleep through and wake up thinking it was all a lovely dream. Her tongue slid into his mouth and he tasted her for the first time. Sweet and delectable, he wanted more. Slowly, he began to respond, ignoring the voice in his head warning him to stop. He kissed her back, long and velvety, delving into her mouth more than he meant to, holding her tighter than he meant to, inhaling her scent more than he meant to.

He felt her stop moving and knew he'd pushed it too far. Slowly, she pulled her head back and stared at him with horrified expression on her face.

"You're not Joe," she said.

## 8

L illy was mortified. Why the hell was she lying on top of Grant Kerridge, kissing him like there was no tomorrow? She jumped off him like he was a poisonous snake.

"I'm sorry," he said immediately. "I was asleep and you..."

She held up a hand, knowing that her cheeks were blood red. She could feel the heat radiating off them. "Stop. I know."

He didn't need to explain. She remembered every vivid detail of her 'dream'. She'd felt his hard body next to her, smelled his manly scent and her muddled, traitorous brain had thought it was Joe. She'd wanted to believe it, wanted it to be him so badly that she'd practically sexually assaulted the guy.

It was only when he'd started kissing her back that she'd realized it wasn't Joe. Joe had been gentle and kind and kissed her like she was the most valuable thing on the planet, like he was afraid she'd break if he'd handled her too roughly, or gripped her too hard.

Grant had no such qualms. His arms had wrapped

around her, holding her close, while his tongue had delved hotly and passionately into her mouth, overriding all her senses and sending her brain into turmoil.

That's when she'd known.

"I thought you were Joe." It was the only explanation she could give, and she hoped to God he'd buy it, else he would think her a terrible tease.

"I know, it's okay." His eyes flickered and she realized he was amused.

"Are you finding this funny?"

He sat up and pulled the blanket over his lap. It was then she realized he had a massive hard-on, not that he seemed fazed by it. The corners of his mouth turned up as he gazed at her. Now, this was more like the Grant Kerridge she remembered.

"You have to admit, it is a unique situation. I didn't think when I fell asleep earlier, that I'd be woken up in such a friendly fashion."

She gave him a hard look, failing to see the funny side. It was mortifying, that's what it was, and disturbing.

"I made a mistake," she said sulkily, refusing to look at him. With his hair all mussed up like that and his blue eyes twinkling at her, she was almost attracted to him. And despite her shock and mortification, she felt this strange desire to kiss him again.

What was that all about?

"Clearly. Anyway, let's not dwell on it."

Easier said than done. She could still smell him on her skin and taste him in her mouth. Her body was tingling where he'd touched her. "I need to wash and brush my teeth," she muttered.

"There's a bucket of water in the corner." He nodded towards the back of the cabin. The amusement faded from his gaze and the smile that she hadn't seen in almost a decade disappeared. She was almost sorry to see it go. He was back to soldier mode.

"I've left some food out for you too, so once you've washed up, you can have a bite to eat. Then we should talk."

"Talk?" She glanced at him nervously. What was there to talk about?

He got to his feet and began folding up the blankets. "Yeah, about our next steps. The evacuation helicopter has gone, but we have several other options."

"Okay."

Phew. For a moment there she'd thought he meant talk about what had happened between them, but that was silly. This was Grant, the SAS soldier and all-round tough guy. He wouldn't talk about anything as sensitive as emotions. She needn't worry about that.

She was upset they'd missed the evacuation, but it was good to know they still had some options. She didn't have a clue what they were, but was confident Grant would explain everything in due course. After all, that was what he did. Survive. Evade. Resist. Extract. She'd heard Joe say it many times, particularly at the beginning of his SAS career.

She sighed. Well, if one had to be captured by enemy forces in Afghanistan, she was grateful she had been rescued by Grant Kerridge. According to Joe, they didn't make them much better than that. And if they had a shot at getting out of here alive, even a remote one, he would find it.

She walked over to the bucket and stuck her finger inside. It was icy cold.

"No heating," was all he said.

No privacy, either. She turned to see whether he was watching her. He was.

"I'll go outside until you're done," he said, and left the cabin without another word.

Left in peace, Lilly stripped down to her underwear, and using the rag and a bar of soap that had been left on the shelf next to the bucket, she got to work. She washed every inch of herself, subconsciously removing all traces of the last few days. The traumatic hike at gunpoint to the village, the fetid mattress, the dirty cave, the escape through the tunnel, and the long walk here. She used one of the military blankets to dry herself. The fibers were harsh and scratched her skin, but she didn't care, she was clean. Then, she shook her clothes vigorously, cringing at the dust that emerged, and got back into them. They were dirty and stained, but there was nothing she could do about that. If they had longer, she'd have washed them too, but there was no way to dry them and she didn't know how long Grant planned to stay here in this cabin. Not for too long, she imagined, not with the Taliban hunting them down like dogs.

It was daytime now. They'd have cleared the rubble from the explosion and realized they weren't in the cave. The only possible way out was the tunnel. By now, they'd be scouring the hills for them, they may even be making their way through the forest. The thought spurred her on.

She gargled with some additional water and rubbed her finger over her teeth, cleaning them as best she could. Toothpaste was not something she'd find in a soldier's pack. Another fact she'd learned from Joe. Apparently, the enemy could smell the minty freshness a hundred meters away.

When she was done she felt a million times better, and the best thing was she could no longer taste or smell him.

## 9

Grant spread the topographical map out over the worn, wooden table with the wonky leg and they both peered over it.

"We're here." Grant pointed to a spot in the middle of a vast, green area. There was no name for it, it was just part of the wider province.

"I had no idea we were so close to a river." Lilly studied the narrow, blue, squiggly line meandering through the valley.

"Yes, it's as wide as the Thames, wider in parts, and at this time of year it will be in flood, thanks to the spring thaw. We don't want to cross it unless we have to."

She nodded but didn't take her eye off the map. As a military software designer, he figured she'd be well versed in reading maps, and he wasn't wrong.

"This is where we have to get to, presumably." She slid her finger down the map to Bagram. "It's over a hundred kilometers away, impossible on foot."

For her perhaps, but he was impressed at how quickly she'd worked out the distance. Bagram Air Base was the closest military base to where they were located, it was also the largest and occupied by the U.S. Military along with the Afghan Armed Forces. Camp Bastion, the ex-British base, was situated much further south near Lashkar Gah, but had now been handed over to the control of the Afghan security forces.

"Sure, so that's Option One. To find some sort of transport to get back to the base undetected. Don't forget we're deep in Taliban territory here, so the villagers will be sympathizers and we will stick out like burning flares, being two westerners."

"With you dressed like you're going into battle," she added, casting a look at his khaki trousers and T-shirt.

He grunted. He'd have his bergen on too but that couldn't be helped. He'd rather be with it than without it. And if they stuck to the off-road areas and skirted the villages, they'd need what was in it for survival. There was no way he was leaving that behind, or his M16 rifle, which even now was slung over his shoulder.

He saw her glance at it in disdain. "Don't you ever take that thing off?"

"No."

He'd have thought she'd known that, after living with a soldier for ten years. One of the first things you were taught in the armed forces was to never let go of your weapon. Even when he slept, he kept one hand on the comforting cold barrel. It was his version of a safety blanket.

"What's Option Two?"

"Option Two is that we head to the nearest village and call the base for an air evacuation. They'd send a chopper and we'd be out of here in no time."

It sounded simple but was actually the more dangerous option. Lilly caught on to that too.

"If we can find someone who'll let us use their phone," she said dryly.

He acknowledged her point with a small nod of his head. "It will be risky walking into a village. We won't know what the reception will be like, or whether we'll even be able to get to a phone."

"Are they all Taliban sympathizers?" She glanced up at him, trying to gauge the risk.

"Not all, but those that aren't will be too scared to help us. We're the enemy in these parts. It's not worth their life to be seen to be cooperating with us, let alone assisting us."

"So they'd kill them for helping us." It was more of a statement than a question. Her expression was one of resolute acceptance. She'd been in the country long enough to know how these things worked.

He nodded.

She shook her head sadly. "Well, at least my system will stop that happening, and once the Afghans have driven the Taliban out of the area, the villagers will get some peace again."

He gave her a sideways glance. "You can't honestly believe it's that simple?"

She shrugged. "No, of course not, but it's something, at least. My software tracks cellphone activity in the province and creates a data map with numbers, frequency of communication and saturation of the area. The Afghan forces can see exactly where the Taliban are hiding."

Impressive. He could see why it was important to keep this software intact and why the Taliban were so keen to destroy it.

"Won't it pick up other cellphone activity too, from non-enemy communications?" It wasn't a criticism, he was just thinking out loud.

"Yes, but in Taliban-held areas, particularly mountainous ones," she raised an eyebrow, "like where we've come from, the probability that it is the enemy is very high. Obviously, there's a margin of error, there always is, but it's minimal in this instance. The troops would have to do an assessment prior to attacking."

She practically glowed with enthusiasm. He could see this project was something she cared very deeply about.

"Even in areas where there's no cellphone reception, they use satellite phones or radio frequencies to communicate. My system picks up on those too, so it's a comprehensive map of all communication activity in any given area."

"Very clever," he acknowledged, then broke into a rare grin. "So we have to protect you at all costs, and prevent the Taliban from getting their hands on you."

She shuddered at the thought of what might happen, what could have happened if Grant hadn't come along when he did. "They'll use me to hack into the system, after which they'll destroy it, or use it to their advantage."

After which, they'd destroy her too. She wouldn't be worth anything once they were in.

"Right, let's get this show on the road. Shall we try for Option B, and if it doesn't work, resort to Option A?"

She thought for a moment. "What would you do, I mean, if I wasn't with you?"

He'd leg it back to Bagram on foot. He could cover a hundred Ks in a couple of days, living off the land, evading capture. It was nothing he hadn't done before, except he didn't say that.

"I'd choose option A. I think it's got a higher success rate. But Option B will be easier for you."

If they didn't get caught.

"Let's stick with Option A, then. I don't want to risk

getting captured again, even if it means we could get home sooner."

He was happy with that.

She looked much better than when they'd first arrived at the cabin. The sleep had invigorated her and the food and being clean again had raised her spirits. He was quietly confident they could make it to the nearest highway where he could hijack a vehicle to get them back to the base. Obviously, road blocks would be a danger, and they'd need to stock up on ammunition. He was running a little low. Luckily, Pat had left some extra ammo in the bergens figuring it wouldn't fit the enemy's AK-47s, although Grant had no doubt they would still have taken it, had they found it.

"This one's for you." He gestured to the second rucksack.

"I wondered about that."' Her eyes roamed over its bulky length with its complicated array of straps, different partitions and assortment of survival paraphernalia that went inside. "Do you think I'll be able to walk with it on my back? It looks huge."

It was huge, weighing fifty pounds when fully utilized, not that she'd have it anywhere near as heavy as that. It would take some getting used to, that's for sure, but she was five foot six or seven and in good health, he couldn't see why she wouldn't be able to carry it.

"We'll make it as light as we can, but I'd recommend taking it. There's a lot of gear in there that we'll need along the way, like food and water, emergency supplies, a sleeping bag."

"Okay," was all she said, but he could read on her face she wasn't sure.

"Let's try it on," he said, once he'd packed it for her. He'd only included the essentials, leaving the heavy stuff like the gas cooker and extra ammo and explosives out to put into his own.

Nervously, she turned her back to him and let him slide it up over her shoulders. He adjusted it, then turned her around to face him. She looked cute with it on, and he nearly smiled, catching himself in time. She wouldn't appreciate it.

He repositioned the padded straps over her shoulders and then fastened the stabilizing strap across her breasts. She kept her eyes fixed on his face, even when his hand grazed her nipple.

"How's that?" he asked, finally meeting her gaze.

She immediately dropped hers. "It's a lot more comfy than I thought." She paced up and down the cabin getting a feel for it. "I think it'll be okay."

"Good."

She might not feel that way after twenty or thirty Ks, but at least she was going to give it a go. He had to admire her guts. So far, she'd been the easiest captive he'd ever rescued, and the sexiest. Mentally, she was sound, feisty even, and she didn't complain, just soldiered on until she was on the point of collapse. She was also an incredible kisser.

## 10

They set out as soon as the sun had set. Lilly was incredibly aware of the weight of the bergen on her back, but she felt quite proud of herself, like she was holding up her own end of this rescue bargain and not being too much of a burden. Whether she could go the distance remained to be seen, but she'd give it her best shot. She had a newfound respect for Grant and Joe, who had lived most of their lives with their bergens on when they were on a mission. It wasn't easy.

She followed closely behind him, marveling at the ease with which he traversed the bumpy forest terrain. He could probably jog it and still not get out of breath. Once again, she could hardly hear his footsteps, while she stomped and stumbled and crunched her way along the invisible path he was taking.

He was dressed in full combat gear, thanks to the supplies his friends had left for them, with his body armor vest and belt-kit over his camouflage fatigues, his rifle in the ready position like he was expecting an attack. The night-vision scope was still attached to his helmet, positioned over one eye, so he could safely lead them through the under-growth. As before, he turned every ten meters or so to make sure she was still behind him.

"You managing?" he asked, after they'd been walking for about a mile.

"So far, so good." She tried to sound upbeat. It was early days still. Grant had mentioned the road was roughly thirty kilometers away, which mean they had about twenty-nine to go.

One step at a time, she repeated to herself while she fixed her gaze on the dark shadowy figure of the SAS soldier in front of her. The moon was even more of a sliver tonight, like a luminous scythe in a field of black. The stars that had been so abundant last night were nowhere to be seen. Perhaps they'd also gone into hiding.

"The cloud cover is good for us," Grant said, once again seemingly reading her thoughts. "This is the most dangerous part of our journey. The enemy will be infil-trating the forest now, they'll be looking for us. They'll know which way we're heading."

"Perhaps we should have taken a different route."' Lilly pointed out.

He glanced sideways at her without breaking his pace. "We still could but it would involve crossing the river, and then crossing it again to get back to the motorway, but if it comes to it, we will."

She realized then he probably would have done if he'd been by himself, but with her, he'd opted for an easier, if more dangerous route.

And what did, 'if it comes to it' mean? If they were attacked?

She swallowed nervously and looked around her, peering into the darkness. The trees seemed to take on human characteristics and branches became rifles pointing at them, the low bushes, crouching Taliban insurgents.

She shivered and focused, once again, on Grant. At least his stealthy physique didn't make her imagination run wild. Well, not in that way, anyway.

She'd always admired his body, not that she'd ever tell him that. She remembered when she'd first met him, how intimidated she'd been by his blatant, physical masculinity. He was also one of the hottest guys she'd ever seen. Raised, for the most part, by a single mother, she'd had a fairly sheltered upbringing. No brothers to jostle with, no father to show her what men ought to be like. Joe had been her first and only love. When her mother had died, Joe had asked her to move in with him and his parents. She'd been sixteen at the time and he'd been her lifesaver. She'd been floundering in a sea of loss and he'd plucked her out to safety. Then she'd met his SAS buddies, in particular Grant with his sexy grin and cocksure attitude, and she'd recoiled. Determined not to like him, and probably a little fearful that he'd take her Joe and turn him into someone rough and ready like him, she'd made up her mind about him before she'd even had a chance to get to know him.

Cocky, arrogant womanizer. That's how she'd pinned him, and for ten years she'd believed it to be true. Looking at him now, however, she began to realize she might have got it wrong. Sure, he was all those things, or had been, but he was also considerate, thoughtful and passionate, traits she had never attributed to him before.

Boy, was he passionate.

She refused to think about that kiss, but even not thinking about it caused her to shiver involuntarily.

On they walked, mile after mile, until finally, much to her relief, Grant called a stop. "Do you need a break?" The eye without the infra-red mechanism attached to it regarded her cautiously.

She nodded, and even though she didn't want to stop, didn't want to be the weak one, she was forced to admit she needed to. Her legs felt like lead and her neck and shoulders ached from the unfamiliar weight of the bergen. Again, she was painfully aware that without her, he would have kept going. Even looking at him now, he wasn't breaking a sweat. His breathing was easy and he seemed totally relaxed. She, on the other hand, was a hot, sweaty mess - and not in a good way.

"If you pop open those buckles, I'll help you take it off," he offered.

She did as he said, and he stood behind her and lowered the rucksack to the ground. She sank down after it, using its lumpy bulk as a welcome backrest.

"Don't get too comfortable." He was still standing and had kept his bergen on. "We can only spare twenty minutes or so, then we'll have to get going again."

"How far have we walked?" She guesstimated at least ten kilometers.

"Six Ks."

What?

Good heavens, how was she ever going to manage this? She took a woeful sip from her water flask and leaned her head back, shutting her eyes.

Grant patrolled the area around her, weaving in and out of the trees, only pausing once to consult the map. The moments ticked by. Now that she knew how exposed they were, she couldn't force herself to relax for more than ten minutes. But she was feeling slightly better, so she got to her feet and attempted to pull the bergen on.

"Here, let me." Grant lifted it up and slid it back on her

shoulders. This time she did up the buckles herself, not meeting his eye. Her nipple tingled in memory of his touch.

"Thanks," she muttered. It was ridiculous that she couldn't put the damn thing on without his help.

"Sh..." He held up a hand.

She froze. Her senses had become fine-tuned to their surroundings but she couldn't hear anything other than the rustle of the leaves and the occasional scamper of a small animal.

Then a twig cracked somewhere behind her in the shadows.

She gasped. "Is it them?"'

He put a finger over his lips, then gestured for her to follow him, and in a half-crouching position melted into the shadows. Worried she'd lose him, Lilly followed close behind. He was so stealthy, if she didn't have him right by her side, she'd have no idea where he was.

They reached a small ditch and Grant gestured for them to climb down into it. There was no talking now. She did what he said, lying flat on her belly, not caring about the damp mud that seeped through her top or the acrid smell of decaying leaves.

He quickly gathered some foliage, ripping off a branch or two with a sudden display of strength and then lay down next to her. He pulled a hessian net out of his bergen's top fold and threw it over them, then he positioned the branches on top of that. They were effectively camouflaged.

"Don't move," he whispered, maneuvering himself into a lying position behind his rifle, the muzzle poking ominously through the netting.

Lilly waited for the inevitable, hardly daring to breathe.

Sure enough, five minutes later she heard footsteps and a small group of insurgents came into view. There were only three of them, thank goodness, but they appeared to be heavily armed. They were searching the woods.

Her heart-rate accelerated. Would they find them? Would she and Grant be gunned down and left to die in this muddy ditch? She tried to keep the horrible thoughts at bay, but she was terrified. Beside her, Grant didn't move a muscle. She couldn't even hear him breathing. His eye was trained into the sights of his rifle, his finger poised over the trigger. Any threat from the three searchers and he'd open fire. She knew he would.

Even though she'd lived with Joe for ten years, she'd never seen him in action. She'd refused to go to any of the military events, not even the pub after a successful mission like the other wives and girlfriends did, which was a long-standing tradition. Joe used to go, of course, and on those nights she knew not to wait up. Sometimes he'd stay over at Grant's and not come home until the next day, something that never sat well with her. As a result of her non-participation, she'd never seen him fire his weapon, not even during a training exercise. And he never talked about his work, none of them did.

How could Grant stay so calm? The insurgents were only meters from them now, one facing in their direction, the other two facing away, but they were moving this way and sooner or later they'd reach the ditch. Still Grant didn't move. No muscle twitch, no flexing, no pent-up anticipation - just a relaxed, controlled body beside her, motionless but lethal, waiting for his opportunity.

One of the men said something in a low voice, and they all stopped. The one closest to them gestured towards the ditch, but the one who'd spoken shook his head and pointed back the way they'd come.

Please go away, she found herself praying. Then we won't have to kill you.

No such luck.

The men continued to approach. They got to the ditch and looked around. The closest one spoke again, it felt like he was standing directly above them. Through the hessian coverage, Lilly could see his foot less than a meter away. If she stuck out her hand she could touch it.

She waited, desperately hoping they'd retreat.

Then the worst happened, the man closest to them stepped into the ditch, his boot clipping Lilly's shoulder. She winced and the man glanced down. With a shout of surprise, he lifted his rifle and pointed it at her.

## 11

Before the insurgent had time to pull the trigger, Grant opened fire and let off a short, sharp volley of shots. The man fell to the ground, the expression of surprise still on his face.

His two colleagues spun around, but once again Grant was faster. He gunned one down with a lethal double-tap before the insurgent had managed to get a shot off. The other man did fire his weapon but he was too enthusiastic and his aim was off. The bullets flew harmlessly over their heads and buried themselves with a dull thud in a tree behind them. Before the insurgent had a chance to bring his weapon under control, Grant shot it out of his hands. Lilly stared in horror at the bloody stumps that remained. Thankfully, the man didn't have time to register the pain before he too was gunned down in another controlled burst of fire.

"Shit!"

Lilly didn't register. She was still in shock from the three men who had dropped dead in front of her.

"Come on. We have to move. The gunfire will have given our position away."

He grabbed the netting and stuffed it back into his bergen. When she hadn't moved, he hissed, "Come on, Lilly. We have to go."

Her eyes were fixed on the dead man.

With a frustrated sigh, he grabbed her hand and pulled her through the forest, zigzagging round trees in a desperate attempt to put some space between them and their previous compromised position.

She followed easily enough, but she wasn't speaking and he could see in her eyes she was still in shock. Unfortunately, there was no time to babysit her now, he had to save their asses.

"I'm heading to the river," he said, between strides. If they could find a way across, they'd have a modicum of safety. It was a lot harder to get an army of Taliban insurgents across a raging river, and many of them couldn't swim. They also wouldn't expect them to go that way. Most people took the path of least resistance.

Grant was running now, pulling Lilly behind him. Her breath came in short gasps, but she was keeping up. He was glad she hadn't fallen completely to pieces. In the aftermath of the shooting, he remembered how shocked she'd been at the dead body of the youngster in the cave. That had probably been her first. Now she'd witnessed three men gunned down in front of her. She'd also probably never had an automatic weapon fired in her ear before. Both the traumatic visuals and the loud noise would be contributing to the shock.

The trees began to thin out, and before long they were in the open air. The dry earth crunched beneath their feet. Up ahead was a patchwork quilt of agricultural fields, well maintained and irrigated from the river. Low stone walls encircled the fields, defining them like in a child's drawing. Grant led Lilly over the first wall, then the second. He could hear the sound of rushing water in the distance. The river wasn't far away now. She stumbled, but his grip on her hand prevented her from falling. With a sob, she came to a stop. It was still dark, so hopefully no one had witnessed their mad dash across the fields. He pulled her down behind the stone wall and put an arm around her.

"Shh... it's okay. We're safe." For a little while, at least.

She was taking overly-deep gulps of air and her eyes were wild and unfocused. She was hyperventilating. He had to get her breathing under control. Without thinking too much about it, he leaned in and kissed her, capturing her mouth with his own. She gave a little moan of protest and tried to push him away, but he held her head securely in place, curving his fingers around the back of her neck. After a few seconds, he felt her relax against him. He felt wetness on his cheeks and realized she was crying silent tears of fear and horror. He wanted to erase the image in her brain, but he couldn't. All he could do was try to take her mind off it, so he kissed her again and she opened under the pressure of his mouth. His tongue slid against hers with a gentle persistence and he was relieved to feel her reciprocate. He kept it light, not delving too deeply, not wanting to startle her any more than she already was. It was hard, because damn, she tasted good. She felt good too, her body was soft and her breasts cushioned against his chest as she leaned in towards him. Then she gave a sob, and flung her hands around his neck. He released her mouth and gave her space to cry. She clung to him, tears pouring down her face for a full minute, before she gave a deep, shuddering breath and got herself under control.

Slowly, he pulled away and studied her face. Her eyes glistened with tears, but weren't glazed over with shock anymore and her breathing appeared to be normal. His approach might have been unorthodox, but it had worked.

"I'm sorry," she sniffed, dropping her arms from around his neck. He'd liked having them there. "I didn't mean to fall apart. It's just... I've never seen anyone shot before yesterday, and now..."

"I know," he said soothingly. "I realize that. I'm sorry It was so sudden, I had no choice. It was either kill or be killed."

She gave a little shake of her head. "I knew it would happen at some point, but I didn't think it would affect me so much."

"It always does the first time."

"Even for you?" She glanced up at him, desperate for consolation.

"Yes, even for me," he said softly, wiping a strand of hair off her face.

"Joe used to have nightmares about it," she said, after a beat.

Grant frowned. He wondered if he'd heard her correctly. She continued, "He used to wake up screaming. Once he even tried to strangle me in my sleep."

"Christ." Grant was appalled. "Why didn't he say anything?" Joe hadn't mentioned he was suffering from nightmares or flashbacks. His performance in the unit had been stellar. If he'd been struggling with PTSD, he'd managed to keep it under wraps.

"He didn't want to be kicked out of the Regiment."

Grant sighed. It would have happened. He would have had to suspend him pending a psyche evaluation. "I had no idea."

She shook her head sadly, "No, I know. He didn't tell anyone. Not even his father."

"Pat would have insisted he get help."

She sniffed. "Exactly."

AFTER A FEW MORE MINUTES, he pulled her to her feet. "You ready to get going again?"

She gave a weary nod, but her gaze flickered down to his lips. He knew she was thinking about his kiss. He was too. And the way she'd clung to him, and her tears.

He forced his thoughts back to the present. "Once we're across the river we can relax for a bit."

They ran across another four fields and climbed over five more low stone walls before they reached the river. It looked like a dark oil slick curving through the landscape. He'd been right, unfortunately, it was running thick and fast. Once they got closer, they could see the surface was covered with white specks rolling over onto each other and hear the loud hissing sound it made as it rushed past.

"You can swim, can't you? In case we end up in the water." He'd never thought to ask.

"Yes."

"Good. Now what we need is a raft of some sort. Perhaps a couple of thin trunks we can tie together."

"Is it too deep to wade across?" she asked.

"Yeah, it will be in the middle. We could swim but we'd get washed downstream by the current and that can be quite scary."

"I'm okay with that." She stood firmly by the riverbank, her eyes glued on the middle section.

"Are you sure? If you get out of your depth and panic in the middle, that could be lethal."

"I used to swim for my school," she told him with the tiniest of smiles. "I also went surfing a couple of times in Cornwall with Joe. I know not to panic in the water."

If she was up for it, he wouldn't need to build a raft and waste any more precious time. As it was, he kept looking over his shoulder, half-expecting the enemy to come charging across the field behind them. Every second counted.

"I'll tie us together using the rope," he said, erring on the side of caution. It wasn't that he didn't believe her, it was just a wild river in the dark was a different story to the beach on a hot summer's day. With her rucksack weighing her down and the powerful current, she'd battle to cross on her own, anyone would.

She nodded, and he took out the rope and tied them together so there was at least four meters between them. Enough to give them swimming space, but short enough to haul her in should she run into trouble. Next, he shrugged off his bergen, took out the sleeping bag, and wrapped it firmly inside a black bin bag.

"Take off your jacket," he said, pulling his off too. She took off the oversized military jacket, compliments of one of his teammates, and handed it to him. He placed it, with his own, inside the plastic bag and tied it firmly. Then, he placed the sealed bag at the top of his pack and refastened the straps. "At least we'll have something warm to get into afterwards."

She glanced nervously at the fast-flowing river, her arms wrapped around her to fend off the biting wind. "The water will be extremely cold," he confirmed with a grimace. "We'll have to get warm quickly on the other side."

She glanced up at him. "Do we take any more clothes off?"

He smiled. "No, now we go in as we are, bergen and all. The plastic bag should keep our jackets dry. Wade in until you can no longer stand then try to swim across the deepest part, but don't be alarmed when you start moving rapidly downstream. I'll pull you across if you get into trouble."

She took a deep breath. "Okay."

So in he went, holding his weapon above the water, feeling the rope tighten around his waist and then slacken again as she followed him in.

This was it.

They had to make it across undetected.

THE WATER WAS FREEZING! Lilly gasped as a million little icicles pierced her legs, then her stomach, then her chest, threatening to squeeze all the breath out of her. Already, her toes had gone numb. She exhaled, long and slow, trying to keep calm. Cornwall had been nothing like this, and that was the North Atlantic, for God's sake.

"You okay?" Grant asked, casting a worried glance in her direction.

I can do this, she chanted as she waded in up to her shoulders. She'd caused him enough hassle over the last hour, she couldn't cop out now. The icy tentacles clawed at her, drawing her in. "I'm okay."

The bank was slippery and her feet felt weird under the water, heavy, but at the same time unable to grip onto the sandy bottom.

"Keep going," he said, his voice calm and steady. "You're doing great."

Despite knowing he was giving her a pep talk, she was grateful for the encouragement. She held onto that as she followed him deeper and deeper towards the fast-moving channel in the center. The current tugged at her legs and she fought to keep her feet on the bottom.

"I think I'm losing my grip," she panted, as every piece of her clothing, her bergen, and her legs threatened to be pulled downstream by the strengthening current.

"Go with it." Grant was a good head taller than her and didn't seem to be having the same problem yet. She was very conscious that when she lost her grip, she'd pull him downstream too.

She took a few more steps, feeling like she was walking on the moon, when the ground disappeared and her legs were sucked out from under her. Immediately, she picked up pace as the current washed her downstream. It was so much faster than she'd realized, and she fought a momentary flicker of sheer panic. Her arms floundered, she tried to put her feet down but went under. Coming up spluttering, she heard Grant say, "Relax and go with it. Swim forward."

So she did. She felt the rope tighten and then Grant was swimming too, big powerful strokes towards the opposite bank. It felt like they were getting nowhere because of how quickly they were moving downstream. The landscape flashed by in a blur. After a few minutes of desperate swimming, she realized they were, in fact, making progress. The rope was taut now, and even though she was swimming her hardest, she knew Grant was doing the bulk of the work. She concentrated on keeping her head above the whitewater, taking deep breaths and moving her arms in a rhythmic motion. After what felt like an eternity, they rounded a bend in the river and the current slowed down. She realized they were on the outside of the meander. Grant found some traction and she felt herself being pulled towards him.

"Put your feet down."

She did, and managed to touch the bottom. A few more

tugs and she was stable again. "We made it," she gasped, relieved that they had got across in one piece. She gazed back up the river for their point of entry, but it was over five hundred meters away and around the bend. Well, at least the men chasing them wouldn't be able to see them anymore.

The realization that they were safe made her legs feel wobbly, or perhaps that was the adrenalin wearing off. She trudged out of the river after Grant, feeling like she was dragging half of it with her. Strangely enough, she was so numb from the cold, that the cold night air felt burning hot against her skin. She mentioned this to Grant who said, "We've got to get you dry."

He untied the rope between them and wound it back around his waist.

"Let's find some cover and we'll get you dry."

"How are we going to do that?" she asked, thinking about the wet blanket and sleeping bag in her rucksack.

He gave her a steamy look. "Body heat."

## 12

L illy was sopping wet and shivering uncontrollably. Her hair was matted and clung to her neck and back and her thin blouse and linen trousers were soaked through. It was imperative he get her warm as soon as possible. He hadn't been joking about the body heat. Lighting a fire was out of the question, since they were not even a mile downstream from their enemy, and both sides of the river consisted of populated farmland. It was best to avoid the lush valley plains if at all possible. Water meant agriculture and agriculture meant people.

But looking at her now, trembling violently, her lips blue with cold, he knew he didn't have much time before hypothermia set in. When he was still in the Regiment, a few tours back, he was on an op behind enemy lines in Iraq with Joe, Rick and Vance. They had been sent in to locate and destroy communication lines when they found themselves in a hostile environment with a faulty radio. There was no way of contacting anyone for an evacuation. Contrary to the weather forecasts, the temperatures had plummeted and they'd purposely left their sleeping bags behind to lighten the load of their bergens, which were already pushing twenty kilos. Because they were in hostile territory, they hadn't been able to light a fire and their tiny gas cookers hadn't done much to relieve the flesh-numbing cold. Rick had actually broken two of his molars because he'd shivered so hard. It was only by cuddling each other and exchanging body heat that they'd managed to survive.

The other problem was their wet clothes. They would only serve to decrease their core temperatures even more. It was essential they get out of them as soon as possible.

He led Lilly across a couple of terraced fields and over yet more stone walls until they reached the outskirts of the farming area. There were traditional mud dwellings dotted over the landscape seemingly at random, but each farmer had erected his house strategically to watch over his farm-land. There was no smoke emanating from any of the chimneys and all of the houses were in darkness given that it was the middle of the night.

"Let's rest up here." Grant led her to where two stone walls intersected to form a sheltered corner that faced away from the chilling wind and towards the start of the tree-covered hills that began their lazy undulations less than a mile away.

"Are these p–poppy fields?" asked Lilly, through chattering teeth. Grant was worried, her body was losing heat faster than she could replace it. That's why she was shivering so violently. It was the body's way of creating energy to warm her up.

"Yeah, as you know, it brings in much more money than any other agricultural crop. The farmers guard their plots obsessively, particularly during the harvest. It's not unusual to see armed guards on patrol."

She peered through the darkness, her brow furrowed with concern.

"I haven't seen anyone yet," he acknowledged, tapping his night-vision scope that he still had positioned over one eye.

Relieved, she shrugged out of her bergen and sunk down against the wall. "I–I don't think I've ever been this c–cold. I can't feel any of my t–toes."

Even her words were stilted and slurred. That was a dangerous sign. Her body was unable to generate heat and was slowing down, affecting her reflexes and coordination. She would continue to cool down unless she got heat from an external source. In freezing conditions, he'd seen soldiers climb into their sleeping bags and be rendered unconscious from hypothermia during the night because their bodies hadn't been able to generate heat themselves. One of the most effective ways to warm someone in that situation was to put them in a sleeping bag with another person with a normal body temperature – and that's exactly what he was going to do. He just wasn't sure how she'd feel about it.

He sat down next to her, his back against the wall, and took off his bergen. Reaching in, he pulled out the sleeping bag and unwrapped it, leaving their jackets inside – they'd need them later once they'd warmed up. Luckily, the bin bag had worked and everything was still dry. He spread the sleeping bag out in front of them, then turned to her. "You're going to have to get out of those wet clothes and climb inside with me."

Their wet clothes were uncomfortable and clung to their damp skin. He desperately wanted to light a fire, but he didn't dare. Not yet. Perhaps when they'd trekked into the hills away from civilization, but that would take time, and Lilly would freeze to death before then.

"What?" He had anticipated her surprise. "Do you mean get undressed and lie inside that sleeping bag with you?"

He shrugged. "It's either that or die of hypothermia. Your body won't heat up on its own. It's going to need mine."

At her exasperated look, he added, "Don't worry. I promise to behave myself. All I want is to get you warm. It's close to zero degrees out here. If we don't get these clothes off they'll freeze around our bodies and trust me, that's not good."

She hesitated, but only for a brief moment, before the cold won out. Turning her back to him, she stripped off her sodden blouse and threw it on the ground. "What about my trousers?"

"They've got to come off too." As if to prove the point, he undid his buckle and let his fall to the ground. He'd already peeled off his fleece and T-shirt while she'd had her back turned. She stared at his nakedness for so long he began to feel self-conscious, which wasn't like him at all. Kicking off his combat pants he climbed into the sleeping bag, placing his weapon and his utility belt containing his knife and handgun next to him, then patted the ground.

Lilly hesitated, her body trembling with cold. She seemed nervous all of a sudden. Was he that scary without his clothes on?

"Come on, Lilly," he said. "This isn't the time for modesty. I'm serious about getting you warmed up. I've lost men to hypothermia before. It happens so quickly and half the time you don't even realize it. Now, please, take them off."

Eyes cast down and with the hint of a blush in her cheeks, she took off her trousers and hung them over her wet bergen in a weak attempt to dry them out and perhaps prolong getting into the sleeping bag with him.

Grant tried not to stare, but Lilly in her underwear was a sight to behold. She had smooth, pale skin and filled out in all the right places. Thanks to the water, he could make out her erect nipples through her bra, and a darker patch hiding behind her white cotton panties.

"You'd better get in," he said, rather huskier than he would have like. Wordlessly, she climbed in next to him and lay down, facing away from him. Their bodies were touching, it was impossible not to in the confined space of the single sleeping bag. She was as stiff and as cold as an icicle. Not wanting to waste any time, he wrapped his arms around her, feeling her tremble against him.

"It's okay," he whispered, drawing her closer until they were spooning. She fit perfectly into the outline of his body. "The shivering will stop soon."

Because his body was cold too, it took a while for him to start generating heat, but he was nowhere near as frozen as her. She felt as frigid as some of the corpses he'd seen on the battlefield. Worried, he cuddled her tightly, absorbing her tremors with his body, and willing his metabolism to kick in. When it did, he felt his body temperature rise and finally, through transference, she began to thaw out.

"Better?" he asked as her tremors began to subside.

"Yes." She huddled against him, desperate to soak up as much body heat as possible. Their position was helping him warm up too, in more ways than one. She fit so snuggly against him with her buttocks rubbing against his groin that he felt himself stir. He shifted position, hoping she hadn't noticed.

Soon, her teeth stopped chattering. The tension drained out of her body as she began to conserve energy rather than expend it. Unfortunately, he could only cuddle her for as long as it took to ward off the hypothermia and get her warm again, then they'd have to move on. If the enemy deduced they'd crossed the river, which was a distinct possibility, they were very exposed lying here naked, less than five hundred meters from the river bank. He glanced up towards the terraced hills. The dense vegetation would offer coverage until they could made it out of the immediate area, then the terrain would change and become rockier and drier the further they got from the river and the higher they climbed into the hills.

"It's working." Lilly turned her head slightly. He couldn't see her full face, only the slant of her neck, the side of her jaw and the gentle rise of her cheekbone. He resisted the urge to bend his head and kiss it.

"I'm glad." He cleared his throat. "Once you've warmed up we should carry on. We need to put some distance between us and the enemy."

"And get to that road," she added.

He nodded. Her hair was drying slowly and soft tendrils swept off her temple and tickled his face. Without thinking, he rubbed his cheek against her head. She snuggled closer, nuzzling her head into the space between his shoulder and his jaw.

His arms squeezed her involuntarily, hugging her closer and he felt his thighs tense to maximize the contact with her legs. In the back recesses of his mind, he was aware that perhaps he shouldn't be enjoying this quite so much, but it felt so right, and they both needed the contact and the warmth.

He wasn't sure of the precise moment when things changed. One minute he was embracing her, enjoying the warmth and the feel of her naked skin against his chest, and the next, there was this sexually charged vibe between them.

Lilly felt it too, and there was a breathless moment when time seemed to stand still.

Slowly and without a word, she turned her head so that he could feel her breath on his neck. He loosened his arms so she could twist around until they were facing each other. It was too dark to read anything in her eyes, but he didn't need to. Her body told him everything he needed to know. She wrapped her arms around him and held him close. He felt her wet bra against his chest, her nipples protruding through the sheer material. He wondered if she could feel his heart racing. The skin on her stomach and thighs were cool against his body, and her legs she intertwined with his.

"Hold me," she whispered.

This wasn't part of the plan, but he was helpless to deny her. Enveloping her in his arms, he tried to ignore the sensations flooding his body.

*She's a hostage*, he told himself. *She's Joe's girlfriend. Not yours.*

Yet, the way she was embracing him made him feel very much like she was his. He sensed her desire and it matched his own. Her lips were so close, and when she began nuzzling him, he couldn't stop himself. He lowered his head and kissed her.

She opened to him straight away, her lips soft and pliable. He kissed her tenderly, exploring her mouth with his tongue. She gave a soft moan, and kissed him back with a surge of desire that surprised him. This wasn't like the kiss he'd given her when she'd been hyperventilating, or how she'd kissed him when she'd thought he was Joe. It was deeper and more personal, he felt the effects reverberate right through his body. Holding her half-naked body in his arms made him appreciate how truly wonderful she was. Again, he wondered how he'd never noticed it before. When he'd met her the first time, she'd seemed so serious and disapproving that he hadn't spared a moment to appreciate anything else about her. He hadn't noticed her flawless skin, her sensuous smile, or her curvaceous figure. Come to think of it, it was probably just as well that he hadn't, seeing as she'd been with Joe at the time and wouldn't have been interested in the likes of him.

He ran his hands down her arms, to her waist and then over the gentle curve of her hips. They came to rest on her bottom and he pulled her towards him at the same time as his tongue delved deeper into her mouth. He felt her dig her pelvis into his, her hands burrowed into his hair. She was completely intoxicating. All he could think of, all he could feel, was her.

This was a completely different sensation to anything he'd felt before. With the other women he'd been with, it had been fun but he'd always known it was a short-term thing, something to keep him occupied while on leave, and because of that, he'd never felt the depth of emotions that engulfed him now. His heart raced, faster than it had when he'd been lying in that ditch waiting for the enemy to spot them, faster than it had during the gunfight in the cave before he'd escaped with Lilly down the tunnel. He realized he had no training for this. Nothing to prepare him for the new and exciting sensations flowing through his body. So he did the only thing he knew how, and kissed her back like his life depended on it.

## 13

Lilly didn't want to think about what was she was doing. All she knew was that she needed it. The freezing water had drained her of any resolve she might have had, and quite possibly even frozen her brain, because she couldn't think of a single reason not to kiss him. His glorious, bare-chested body was wrapped protectively around her, she could feel his legs touching hers, his heart beating in his chest and the delicious ministrations of his tongue. It had been so long since she'd been held like this, that she'd almost forgotten how comforting it was. Any guilt she may have felt about betraying Joe's memory had been washed away by the frigid river water and her desperate need for warmth.

Grant made her feel safe, there was no doubt about it. He had that way about him. Confident, tough and capable. More than capable. He knew how to survive out here in the freezing wilderness, he knew how to evade the enemy, and he knew how to get her back to safety - plus he looked good doing it.

As she kissed him, matching his passion with her own,

she felt herself being drawn deeper and deeper into his presence. He was a commanding personality, whether it was strutting arrogantly around the base like when she'd first met him or stalking stealthily through the undergrowth without making a sound. Either way, you always knew he was there and in control of the situation. He was the one people watched, the one they followed. The one Joe had followed. But she didn't want to think about that now. Her need to feel safe and protected was stronger.

Heat flooded into her body and all her senses snapped to attention. His stubble felt erotic against her chin, his hand buried in her hair made her tingle with excitement. She loved the way he held her against him with no room to escape, like he knew she wouldn't want to, like he didn't want her too. She heard him growl in the back of his throat and felt a rush of pleasure that he was enjoying this as much as she was, that she had the power to turn him on – and boy was he turned on. His rock-solid manhood dug into her hip, hinting at the possibilities.

Her arms clung to his neck and she held on for dear life as he kissed the cold and fear away. His passion removed the horror of her abduction and the memories of the three men he'd shot and replaced it with delicious, life-affirming emotions that flowed through her body and warmed her from head to toe.

When their kiss reached explosive proportions and Lilly felt like she was about to self-combust, Grant broke away, breathing hard. "Lilly," he rasped, staring at her with a mix of desire and confusion. "What's happening?"

"I don't know," she whispered, looking deep into his eyes. She barely knew her own mind right now. Her body was on fire, and she longed for his touch, to feel him inside her. "Does it matter?" she asked, reason deserting her, even though deep down she was aware that this had gone way beyond the basic necessity for warmth.

"Of course it matters," he said, concern flashing across his face, but he didn't release her. She could still feel his breath on her skin. "I'm supposed to be protecting you, looking after you." He paused and glanced down at her lips, his eyes feverish. "Not this."

It was almost impossible to break away. His body was pushing into hers in all the right places. Then, he took the matter out of her hands. "I think you're warm enough," he muttered. "We should probably get going."

Lilly squeezed her eyes shut. She'd gone and done it again, practically sexually assaulted him. What was it with this guy? To be fair, he was half-naked beside her, and with his glorious torso, abs that a GQ model would be proud of, and powerful thighs from tabbing across hostile territories, it was a lot to ask to keep her hands to herself.

With a small sigh, she sat up, creating some distance between them. Immediately, the warm space in the sleeping bag was flooded with cold night air, which helped cool her ardor. He was right. She'd let her desire to feel safe run away with her. He'd drawn her in through no fault of his own and for some primitive reason, she hadn't been able to resist. But, he had a job to do, a mission to complete. They couldn't afford to let anything interfere with that.

She pushed herself away from him, her heart heavy. For a brief moment she'd felt happy again, like all was right in the world, which was ridiculous considering where they were and the treacherous situation they were in. That was the effect Grant had on her. She shook her head, the cold water must seriously have frozen her brain.

"I'm sorry." She wrapped the sleeping bag around her nakedness as he climbed out. "I don't know what happened.

One minute you were keeping me warm and the next..." She didn't need to elaborate, she could see by his expression that he understood. It had felt so natural, like an extension of his protective duty towards her and it had happened so fast that she hadn't had time to think.

But, she also saw confusion in his eyes. The heat hadn't entirely dissipated, but it was fast being replaced with something that looked suspiciously like guilt.

"It's not your fault," he said, letting her go. "I overstepped the mark."

There was that ingrained military discipline stepping in to save the day. It was good of him to take the blame but she couldn't help feeling a little disappointed. Was that all it was? He'd got carried away? She supposed one half-naked woman in Grant Kerridge's arms was the same as any other.

"Well, let's pretend like it didn't happen." Her tone was more clipped than she would have liked. Her vulnerability annoyed her. One minute she'd been clinging to him like her life depended on it, and in all fairness, it probably had. The next, she was upset that he'd come to his senses before she had. And he was perfectly right, of course, he was there to do a job. The operation was to rescue her, and he wouldn't jeopardize that by allowing himself to get carried away.

His expression turned neutral, like all the emotions had suddenly been switched off, a handy trait when on a mission. That's what she was. His mission. "It's probably best," he said, pulling his wet pants on. She watched while he got his jacket out of the bag and put that on too, then tossed her the other one, avoiding eye contact. "You'll have to wear the same trousers, but this should keep you warm and dry.

She grabbed her clothes and got dressed, then rolled up

the sleeping bag and stuffed it back into the bag. They'd be crossing the river again further down. She made a mental note not to get hypothermia again, the consequences were too intense.

"If you feel up to it, we should get going." His utility belt was back on now, and he'd slung his rifle over his shoulder.

He made to help her with the rucksack but she shook her head. "I can manage."

It took considerable effort, but she succeeded in hoisting the thing up and swinging it onto her back. She'd be damned if she'd let him help her anymore. From now on, there would be no contact between them, it was too dangerous. For some reason, she couldn't control herself around him. When he touched her, she wanted more.

It suddenly became clear what had happened when she'd first met him, ten years ago. She'd felt it then, the power of his attraction, and it had frightened her. She remembered meeting him on the base, he'd been in jeans and a T-shirt, off duty. He'd grinned at her, his blue eyes sparkling with vitality and mirth, then shaken her hand, holding it that little bit longer than was necessary. Then a blonde woman in a tank-top and skinny jeans had sauntered up behind him and put an arm possessively around his waist. He'd kissed her, full on the lips, right in front of them, causing her to blush and look away. She'd been very naive back then, only eighteen and barely out of secondary school. His blatant sexuality had disturbed her, and she'd made up her mind to disapprove of him, right then and there.

Not only that, but she'd also feared his influence over her boyfriend. Joe admired Grant and looked up to him. What if Grant's cavalier attitude and arrogance rubbed off on her Joe, and led him astray? Then she'd lose the only definite thing in her life, the only man she could depend on. Consequently, she'd done all she could to keep Joe away from him. It was impossible, given they were in the same unit, but after hours, when he wasn't at work, she'd kept Joe to herself, integrating him into her friendship group, refusing to socialize with his teammates.

This new revelation made her decidedly uneasy, the acknowledgment that Grant had this strange power over her. Especially since it hadn't been reciprocated. Back then, she hadn't had the same effect on him as he'd had on her. That day at the barracks, he'd said how good it was to meet her and had disappeared with his blonde without so much as a backward glance, while she'd stared after him, filled with a sense of foreboding.

She watched Grant sweep the ground with his foot, eradicating any sign that they'd been there. Then he swung his much heavier bergen onto his back and adjusted the straps, his weapon sandwiched between his legs. It was never far away from his body, never out of reach, always connected to him like an extension of himself.

The only time he'd put it down had been when he'd been kissing her.

## 14

They followed the tree line south as best they could. The ground was rugged and uneven, with lots of clumps of vegetation and long grass growing between the trees, which made walking difficult. On top of that, they were constantly hiking at an angle which made them feel lopsided. Grant was used to it from previous tours, but Lilly was taking the strain. Each mile took the better part of an hour.

Every now and then they'd move deeper into the vegetation to avoid a dwelling or group of dwellings. The simple, rectangular houses hung precariously to the steep hillside like a stack of matchboxes positioned on top of one another. If something happened to the bottom one, they'd all fall down.

Grant glanced worryingly at the sky. It was getting lighter faster than he would have liked. Soon it would be daybreak and they'd have to take cover, for it would be too dangerous to continue. The hillside and indeed the lush valley plains were filled with shepherds, farmers, fishermen and any number of people during the day. Lilly, who was a few steps behind him, said, "How long have we got?"

He liked how she caught on to what he was thinking so quickly. "Half an hour at the most."

She didn't reply, but picked up her speed which he knew must have required effort. On top of her exhaustion, all the items in their bergens were now wet, which would add additional weight, and they hadn't eaten for hours.

"As soon as daylight breaks we'll hole up and eat something." She gave a nod, like talking was too much effort. Her hair was completely dry now, but the tendrils at her temples clung damply to her forehead. He too was perspiring despite the coolness of the early morning, but it beat being freezing cold. It seemed in this place there was no in-between.

They trudged on until Lilly began stumbling. That was his cue that she was too exhausted to continue. He began looking around for a place to camp for the day. They needed to be completely out of sight from anyone who might happen to walk past. Eventually, he stumbled upon a clump of trees that grew closely together providing all-round coverage like a green circular hedge. Their roots intertwined in the middle making natural armchairs for them to sink into.

"This is it," he said, helping her into the middle. At first it looked like she was going to refuse his hand, but then weariness overcame her and she let him help her in.

It bothered him that she was acting so offish since their kiss, but he knew it was probably for the best. She was dangerous for him and she was off-limits. Pat would freak out if he knew what had happened. Joe's girlfriend, and he couldn't control himself in her presence, but when he'd held her in his arms it had felt so right. There was no other way to explain it. When she'd turned her face up to his, he hadn't thought twice. And he'd enjoyed every minute of it, there was no point in denying it. Did that make him a bad person? A bad friend?

He shook his head and got busy setting up camp. It didn't matter what he thought – he could analyze the hell out of it later – but right now he couldn't afford to lose focus. He took Lilly's bergen off her back and set it aside. She sat down with a grimace, but didn't moan. She never moaned despite the fact that she must be shattered. She looked it, the purple circles beneath her eyes more enhanced, her cheeks pale and blotchy, her eyes slightly glazed.

"Why don't you get some sleep?" he suggested, as the sun poked its head over the horizon.

She nodded and leaned back against a tree trunk.

"Here, use this as a pillow." He grabbed the blanket out of his pack and handed it to her. She rolled it up and positioned it under her neck with a grateful smile. She closed her eyes and a few minutes later she was asleep.

He took out the sodden sleeping bag and hung it out in the trees above them, making sure it wasn't visible from outside their little circle. The temperature rose with the sun, getting higher as the morning wore on. Grant kept vigil outside the circle of trees while Lilly slept. He kept his weapon on his lap and enjoyed the sensation of the sun on his face.

It was almost noon when Grant heard voices. He frowned and got to his feet, careful not to make a sound. He listened carefully. Questions flooded into his mind as he assessed the situation, questions he'd been trained to ask. Where were they? How many of them? Were they a threat?

The trees and foliage had a way of distorting sound so it was hard to pinpoint their exact location, but he thought there were two of them. Two distinct voices talking in an Arabic dialect he didn't recognize. That didn't mean they weren't dangerous, however. In these mountains, there were so many different rural communities and tribes, that dialects varied greatly from one area to the next. These men could be Taliban insurgents, or sympathizers, or even harmless farmers who felt it was in their best interests to share what they knew about the whereabouts of two westerners on the run. Crouching low, he went to investigate, following the voices as they ricocheted off the trees. Five minutes later he had a visual. Yes, he was right, two turbaned men in flowing robes having a smoke. He crouched down and watched for a while, thinking that if they moved on, away from their hiding place, it might be okay. Unfortunately for them, they didn't. As they turned in the direction he'd come from, Grant noticed an AK-47 hanging off the one man's shoulder. It had been hidden amongst his robes which is why he hadn't seen it straight away.

His mind cleared with only one thought present.

Neutralize.

In a slow, deliberate movement, he slipped his fighting knife out of its leather sheath and tracked the men silently through the woods like a leopard circling its prey. One of the men flicked his cigarette butt on the ground, said something to his friend, and disappeared around a tree to take a leak. Grant watched as he leaned his weapon against a tree.

Big mistake.

He snuck up behind him, put a hand over his mouth, and slit his throat in one short, aggressive swipe. The man made a soft gargling sound before he sunk to the ground. Grant supported his weight to prevent any noise, then he went in search of the other one.

This guy was pacing back and forth, clearly agitated. He

shouted for his friend, but got no reply. Making an annoyed sound at the back of his throat, he went looking for him.

Grant followed.

Before the man even saw the lifeless body of his friend, he pounced, giving the insurgent the same treatment. This man didn't utter a sound.

Grant cleaned the blood off his knife with a bunch of leaves before holstering it, and then set about clearing up the bodies. He didn't want to leave any trace. There was a large bush nearby with dark, succulent leaves not unlike holly. He crawled inside and began hollowing it out. When he was done he threw the AK-47s on the ground then stashed the bodies on top of them. Finally, he stuck the leafy branches around the edges to provide extra camouflage. He inspected his handiwork. No one would ever believe there were two bodies inside, not until they began to rot and the smell attracted attention.

Still, their position had been compromised. These two might be missed and he didn't want an army of insurgents combing the woods for them. It was time to move on. He went back to the camp to wake Lilly.

## 15

"Why are we leaving?" Lilly asked Grant, as she fell into step beside him. The sudden awakening had left her a bit disoriented. Ten minutes ago she'd been in dreamland and now they were trudging along the hillside again, zigzagging round tree stumps and foliage, and tripping over hidden roots and anthills. Well, she was tripping, he was doing his usual Rambo thing.

"I told you. I heard voices and thought we'd better head out. Our position there was no longer safe."

"Did you see anyone?" she asked.

"Here, eat this." He handed her an energy bar. "It should keep you going until I can find us somewhere else to camp, then you can have some of the rations."

She took the energy bar. Rations would be good, she was ravenous. She could barely remember the last time she ate, it was so long ago. She'd been sipping her water regularly, though, to ward off dehydration. She wasn't going to allow that to happen again. They carried enough water between the two of them to last three days, if they were careful. But she was conscious that she was drinking way more than Grant. He hadn't slept either, and by the looks of him, he could do with a nap. His eyes were permanently narrowed while he squinted through the trees on constant alert for the hidden enemy, but she could see the telltale dark circles beneath them. He was also sporting the beginnings of a beard, which annoyingly only served to make him appear more manly. She didn't like beards as a rule. Joe had always shaved his off when he got back from an op, but then he'd had ginger hair and beards didn't suit him. Grant didn't have that problem. His thick, brown hair was flecked with golden strands which caught the light when he stepped out from beneath a tree, and his beard was the same, albeit a shade darker. She'd felt his stubble on her jaw earlier that morning after their little swim, and it had turned her on more than she cared to admit. If she closed her eyes, she could still feel it scratching her skin when she kissed him.

She took her annoyance out on the wrapper, making a loud rustling noise as she scrunched it up. Grant flashed her an irritated look.

Oops, they were so completely alone in the woods, she'd forgotten they needed to be quiet. With an apologetic smile, she pocketed the wrapper and tried to be stealthier. It was hard walking with one foot higher than the other and her bottom leg was beginning to ache. Determinedly, she gritted her teeth and kept going.

After an hour, they came to a dilapidated pile of stones that looked like it might once have been a dwelling of some sort. The back wall was half-standing, but the top had toppled forwards onto the rest of the rubble. It was surrounded by vegetation, some of it growing up through the cracks in the rocks, slowly claiming back its territory.

"Wait here."

She did as she was told while Grant did a lap of the ruins and then returned, satisfied they were uninhabited. "It'll do. We can rest up here for a bit."

She followed him behind the structure and sat down, shrugging off her bergen once she was on the ground. It was easier to remove this way, and didn't require any assistance. Unfortunately, it didn't work in reverse, since she couldn't get up with it on her back.

"Why don't you take a nap?" she said, seeing him suppress a yawn.

He glanced at her and shook his head. "I'm okay."

"Don't be silly. You haven't slept since yesterday. I don't want a zombie protecting me if we come under attack." At his sardonic look, she added, "Don't worry, I'll wake you at the first sign of danger."

Eventually, he relented. "Give me an hour," was all he said before he lay back against his rucksack, rifle on his lap, and shut his eyes.

Wow. That was quick. She wished she could fall asleep so fast. It usually took her ages.

Left to her own devices, she took the opportunity to relieve herself, then assumed a position where she could see in all directions, but was out of the line of sight in case anyone should come wandering through the clearing.

The sun was deliciously warm and she tilted her face up to it, marveling how different the day temperatures were from the night. This really was a country of extremes. Her clothes were completely dry now, including the sleeping bag, which was rolled up and back in her bergen. She knew they'd have to cross the river again and probably at night, which she was not looking forward to, but Grant had said access to the motorway was that side, so they had no choice.

She admired the tiny creatures scurrying around amid

the stones, oblivious to the plight of the westerners using their environment as a makeshift camp. A squirrel or something similar with a bushy tail whipped across the clearing and into a crevice, carrying a nut in its mouth. She sat stockstill, watching and listening to the sounds of the leaves rustling and the branches creaking around her.

She estimated almost an hour had gone by when she heard gentle tinkling sound. Frowning, she sat up a little straighter and listened a little harder. There it was again, definitely a bell tinkling. She got up and dashed back to where Grant was sleeping. She poked him on the shoulder and immediately he opened his eyes and said, "What's up?"

"I heard something, a bell, I think."

He jumped to his feet, positioned his rifle against his shoulder and peeked around the stone wall. Lilly, who was amazed he could come to so fast, froze as the bell sounded again.

"There!"

"Wait here," Grant said for the second time that afternoon, and disappeared around the corner.

Lilly didn't move a muscle. A moment later he was back, an annoyed expression on his face. "It's a goat herder," he whispered.

"Oh." That was okay then. How dangerous could a goat herder be?

"Get down," whispered Grant, as footsteps could be heard approaching the pile of stones.

They both crouched down behind the wall. Grant, his rifle over his shoulder, peered through a crack while Lilly prayed the shepherd would go away.

He didn't.

Whistling, he sat down on the wall and lit a roll-up cigarette which he took from behind his ear. Without a sound, Grant unsheathed his knife. The goat herder had no idea that Grant was less than a meter behind him.

Lilly stared at the knife in alarm. Was he seriously going to kill the guy?

She shook her head violently, but Grant ignored her. He was totally focused on the man sitting on the wall. There was a loud baa, and the sound of bells ringing. The goats were gathering around him, no doubt pulling the tufts of grass out from between the cracks in the stones.

Lilly could smell the smoke from his cigarette as she squatted against the wall, her eyes riveted on Grant. His face was a mask of concentration. He didn't waver, he stood like a wax figure at Madam Tussaud's with his arms outstretched in front of him, the knife glinting in his right hand.

The goat herder leaned back and for a moment, Lilly thought Grant was going to react. She grabbed his arm and shook her head violently.

"No," she mouthed.

He scowled at her and shook off her hand, but did pause. The herder jumped down off the wall and went to see to his goats. A few minutes later, they heard him walking away, still whistling to himself. Lilly only relaxed when the sound of the bells could be heard fading into the distance.

## 16

"Don't ever grab my arm like that again." Grant was furious. "That guy was a threat, I was about to neutralize him. By stopping me, you put both of us in danger."

"From that guy? He was a harmless goat herder."

"Until he gets home and mentions to his mates that he saw two foreigners up in the hills. The word gets back to the insurgents and before you know it we have an army hunting us down on this side of the river too."

Lilly thought about that, then said, "But he didn't turn around. He didn't see us, so there was no reason to neutralize him."

Grant shook his head. "Let's hope you're right."

"What? You think he could have been pretending?"

Grant shrugged. 'Yeah, I think anything is possible, that's why I don't take chances."

"Violence isn't always the answer, you know." She glared at him. "There are other ways to resolve conflict."

"Not out here," snapped Grant. Even now that goat

herder could be racing back to tell his friends how close he came to getting his throat slit by an enemy soldier. It would make a good drinking story. "Do you think if we'd asked that guy nicely not to tell anyone we were here, he would have listened?"

"Maybe." Her defensive expression belied her words.

"Don't be naive. It would be in his best interests to tell what he saw, that way he'd ingratiate himself with the Taliban."

"But he didn't see us," Lilly reemphasized.

Grant clenched his jaw. "It's still not worth the risk."

They marched on in silence after that, Grant in front and Lilly a few steps behind. He wanted to put as much distance between them and this place as possible. He had a niggling feeling that that goat herder wasn't as harmless as he'd seemed, and in situations such as these, he'd learned to trust his instinct. He hoped Lilly was right, and he was worrying for nothing, but that little voice in his head wouldn't go away.

The landscape changed as they walked south. The valley curved along with the meanders in the river and the lush vegetation on either side shrunk and expanded depending on which side the floodplain was. The forest thinned out and turned into low-lying shrubs and bushes, which meant less coverage for them. Grant, fearing a reprisal from the goat herder and uncomfortable travelling during the day, set a grueling pace. There was something about the guy that bothered him, but he couldn't put his finger on it. Perhaps it was his whistle. It had been too contrived, too deliberate. On the other hand, maybe he was imagining things, but he didn't want to take a chance.

He could hear Lilly panting behind him as she struggled

to keep up. Typically, she hadn't asked him to slow down, or complained about the speed. He respected her for that, and ideally, he wanted to hike five kilometers south before they stopped to await the fall of darkness, but he didn't think she'd make it. After three, he held up a hand. Relieved, she sank down on a small tree stump. It was blisteringly hot and her face was flushed. She had droplets of perspiration on her face and neck. He too was sweating up a storm, although he was used to it. In the Summer months, mid-afternoon temperatures in this country could soar to forty or even fifty degrees Celsius, but right now the mercury was probably hovering around thirty. It was still hot enough to do damage, which was another reason why he preferred travelling at night. Luckily, down here in the valley it was a bit cooler, but he still took a cap out of his bergen and offered it to Lilly. "Here, wear this. It'll keep the worst of the sun off your face until we can find shelter."

Wordlessly, she took it and put it on. They had a drink while he studied the map. "If we move to higher ground, we might be able to find a small cave or crevice to shelter in for the rest of the day. Then we can move out once the sun's set."

She nodded, not making eye contact. She was still upset with him, but he stood his ground. He might not be as smart as her when it came to computers, but out here, he was the expert, and while he didn't condone killing people unneces-sarily, he recognized a threat when he saw one. With his mouth in a grim line, he gestured for her to get up. "Let's move out."

The next two kilometers were at a steady angle uphill. It was tough going, and he slowed his pace so Lilly could keep up. The ground beneath their feet changed from spongy grass and clumps of foliage to dry dirt and pebbles the higher they climbed. It made traversing the hill difficult and he had to take Lilly's hand to prevent her slipping and sliding on the gravel. He was also highly conscious that they were visible from the valley below by anyone with a pair of binoculars. He had to get them undercover as soon as possible.

"Here," he said, spying a vertical rock crevice that was wide enough for both of them to lie in. The shadow it created would protect them from prying eyes below, and it would shelter them from the harsh sun until darkness fell.

Relief flashed across Lilly's face and he felt a twinge of guilt for pushing her so hard. "We'll be safe here for a while," he said, letting go of her hand.

She practically fell down and shrugged off her rucksack. He handed her a water flask, which she took gratefully. After surveying the area and feeling relatively secure that they were safe and out of sight, he sat down next to her.

"Look, I'm sorry about earlier. It might seem harsh to you, but I was doing my job."

"Do you enjoy killing people?" she asked, turning to face him.

He narrowed his eyes. "What's that supposed to mean? Of course not, but sometimes it's necessary." That's why he was here. In his job, it was almost always necessary.

Lilly studied his face. "Do you really think that was necessary, back there? That man was innocent. He wasn't even carrying a weapon. How could you condone killing him?"

Grant shook his head. It wasn't what he'd done, it was what he could or would do next. The consequences of letting that man live could be detrimental, even deadly.

"It's always a tough choice when something like that happens." He sighed and leaned back against his bergen. "You've got to do a risk assessment and make a split-second decision. I did that."

"And you decided to kill him."

He gave a curt nod. "Yes. I thought he'd seen us." He suddenly knew what had been bugging him. "He left without finishing his cigarette."

That gave her pause.

"Are you always so suspicious of people?" she said, leaning back beside him.

He stared straight ahead, but he was conscious of her closeness. "In enemy territory, yes. Are you always so trusting?"

She had the grace to chuckle. It cleared the tension from the air. "Not always, but there are some people I trust implicitly, or rather did."

"Like Joe?" He gave her a sideways glance.

She looked down at her hands. "Yes, I knew Joe would always be there for me and Pat. When my mother died, Joe asked me to move in with him, and his parents sort of adopted me. They were wonderful, I owe them so much."

"It was Pat who asked me to come and get you." Grant told her. "He was so worried about you."

She nodded. "He's like a father to me, a real sweetie."

Grant thought of the barrel-chested, bear of a man and laughed. "I haven't heard Pat described quite like that before."

Lilly said softly. "And, I trust you."

He glanced at her, surprised.

She continued, "I know you'll do everything you can to get me home safely, and I'm incredibly grateful. You didn't have to come here. After what happened to Joe, I'm surprised you did."

"I owed it to Joe," was all he said.

"You're a good friend," she whispered, and leaned across to kiss him on the cheek.

He gazed at her for a long moment. "Lilly, I..."

"Shh..." she said moving closer. "Just kiss me."

## 17

L illy pulled his head gently toward hers. She could see the hesitation, the uncertainty in his gaze and knew it was because of Joe. Grant was loyal to his friend, which was why he was here, putting his life on the line for her.

But she needed him now. She needed him to kiss away the fear and the weariness and make her feel safe again. It was addictive, the protection that he offered. A powerful man, he could kill someone with his bare hands as effectively as with his combat knife or his assault rifle. He held the power of life and death over the unsuspecting enemy, over anyone they came into contact with, over her. It both excited and terrified her.

She kissed him, gently at first, coaxing his lips open. He shut his eyes momentarily, then opened them again and looked at her.

"I'm not sure this is such a good idea," he whispered.

"Why not?" She continued to kiss him along his jaw bone.

"Joe loved you," he murmured.

She glanced up at him. "I know he did, and I loved him, but this isn't about Joe. This is about you and me." She moved on to his neck.

He groaned. "Besides, Pat would kill me if he found out."

Lilly whispered, "Then, he doesn't need to find out."

Her desire to be wrapped in Grant's arms and kissed passionately like they had at the river was overwhelming. She was so tired of being scared, she needed him to erase the ugliness of the goat herder incident, and the men chasing them. For a short while she wanted to forget where she was, and relish who she was with. She was done fighting her attraction towards this man. He'd affected her from the day they'd met, and right now she wanted to embrace that. If this experience had taught her anything, it was life was too short to hold back. Anything could happen. They might not even make it to the motorway, they might die tonight crossing the river – and she didn't want to go without savoring him one last time. Properly.

"Please, hold me?"

That was all it took. Grant slid his hand around the back of her head and pulled her towards him, as his lips crushed into hers. The forcefulness took her breath away. Yes! This was what she wanted. His passion would drive out her demons and make her feel safe again.

She kissed him back hard, opening herself up to him. He pushed her gently down onto the ground and ravished her mouth, a hand behind her head to protect it from the hard, cave floor. He was still thinking about her, even in the heat of the moment. His other hand caressed her cheek, then slid down her neck and over her blouse. It settled on her breast and she arched into him, wanting him to touch her. He squeezed gently, sending electric charges radiating through her body. Spurred on by her response, he didn't hesitate to slip his hand under her blouse and cup her bra, which miraculously, was still in one piece after the river swim. She hadn't taken it off as she figured she might need the support with all the hiking and climbing and running away from the enemy that they were doing. But right now all she wanted to do was rip it off.

He took care of that for her, reaching behind her as she arched to give him access, and unclipped it. The feel of his rough hand on her tender breast was intoxicating. She gasped, and opened her eyes to look at him. He stared down at her too, the heat in his gaze made her flush with anticipation. Joe had never looked at her like that.

She knew it was wrong to compare, but Grant was so different. Joe had looked at her like she was a delicate porcelain doll, a fact that had annoyed her at times, but she hadn't known why. She knew now. She didn't want to be treated like she might break. She wanted to feel the raw passion of reckless abandon. This sexual frenzy was something she'd never experienced before. It astounded her, and she was amazed she even had it in her. She was so used to Joe's gentle administrations.

She wanted more, so she reached for Grant again, and pulled him back into a kiss.

GRANT IGNORED the voices in his head telling him to stop. He wanted her too, desperately. Part of him was aware that Lilly's need was born out of a desire to feel safe and protected, perhaps even to distract herself from the seriousness of their situation, but the other part of him didn't care. He could sense her frantic need and it matched his own. If he were honest, he'd wanted this since the moment she'd climbed over him to freedom in the tunnel.

He grabbed a blanket from the top of his bergen and positioned it under her head, then ran both his hands over her body, exploring every mound and curve. She was amazing, so soft and sensual. As he kissed her, he felt himself drowning in her scent and her taste and her touch. He caressed her over her trousers, once again feeling the lace of her panties through the thin cotton material. It drove him mad.

He broke away, glancing at her face and thinking he'd never met anyone so beautiful. Her head was back, her dark hair splayed over the cold, hard cave floor. Her lips were parted and she was breathing heavily. He watched as she opened her eyes to look at him. They burned with an emerald flame, and he held her gaze as he unbuttoned her trousers and slipped his hand beneath her panties. She gasped and thrust upwards trying to maximize the contact. He massaged her, marveling at how responsive she was.

God, he wanted her.

Maintaining his control, he stroked her gently and rhythmically, loving the feel of her beneath his fingers. Her breathing got quicker and quicker, and then he felt her convulse beneath him as she found release.

Seeing her orgasm turned him on so much, it was almost painful, and he strained against his underwear. He kissed her gently as she recovered, thinking that perhaps that second river crossing wasn't such a bad idea after all. He could do with cooling down.

When she opened her eyes, he was moved by the tenderness in them. No one had ever looked at him in that way before.

She touched his face. "Thank you. I needed that."

He grinned like a schoolboy. "Glad to be of service."

Then she gave a knowing smile and reached down

between his legs. He was half-lying on top of her, with one leg positioned between hers, which gave her easy access. He closed his eyes as he felt her hand rub him over his combat pants. It felt so good, he didn't want her to stop.

To his surprise, her hands went to his belt and she started to undo the buckle.

He gazed at her. "Are you sure?" A mountain cave wasn't the most romantic of places.

"I've never been surer of anything in my life," she whispered, as his belt popped loose. "Grant, I want to feel you inside me."

Once he heard those words, he was lost. With a groan, he pulled his trousers down enough so that the important bits were free, then he undid hers. She wriggled them off her hips and pushed them down to her knees. Neither of them dared take off any more clothing in case they had to leave in a hurry. As it was, Grant felt uncomfortable being so vulnerable, but his weapon was right beside him and his need to make love to Lilly had taken temporary priority. She was all he could think about.

He positioned himself on top of her, sensing her urgency. There was no foreplay, no tender words or caressing, they were too far gone for that. Her hand folded around his shaft and guided it in. She gasped as he entered her, and for a moment they lay still, gazing into each other's eyes and relishing the sensation.

Then, the urgency returned and he thrust into her and she arched up towards him with a throaty groan. He captured her mouth with his and they kissed as their rhythm built. She clung on to him, locking them together, as he thrust more deeply. He could feel her muscles clenching around him, driving him on.

It wasn't romantic. It was fast and dirty, and insanely dangerous. But it felt wonderful.

Oh, God. He was going to lose it.

His fabled SAS control went out the window as she dug her nails into his back and tightened around him. She cried out in ecstasy, her body convulsing as her orgasm hit.

He gave one final thrust, then exploded inside her. He held her tightly as the waves of passion washed over him, then with a groan, collapsed next to her. She was still hanging on to him, soaked in perspiration.

"Oh, my God," she said, gazing at him in wonder. "That was amazing."

"Tell me about it." He was still getting his breath back.

"I can't believe I had sex with you in a cave."

He laughed. "It's a first for me, too."

She ran her hand down his arm, making his hair stand on end. "So you don't behave this way with all your hostages?"

He tilted his head to look at her. "No, just you."

She smiled. "I'm relieved to hear it."

## 18

G rant let Lilly sleep as he studied the map. His body was still glowing from their love making, but he was also berating himself for his lack of control. He was here to protect her, for Joe's sake, not have sex with her. Although, deep down he knew it was a lot more than sex. He wasn't ready to analyze it yet, but his feelings for Lilly were different from anything he'd ever felt before. He glanced out over the darkening valley with its tangle of vegetation and wondered how many insurgents were combing it right now, searching for them.

The river was at its narrowest two klicks south. That would be the best place to cross. Maybe there'd be a raft or a boat he could steal so Lilly wouldn't have to get soaked again. He frowned at the map. There was also the worry that during the river crossing they'd be vulnerable to an ambush. The valley narrowed at that point, which made the river easier to cross, its base becoming rockier and more uneven. On the banks, there was less vegetation and fewer places to hide. The rocky outcrops on the steep valley sides also provided excellent cover for snipers. Under normal circumstances, he'd head south for another ten klicks before crossing, but that would result in a more difficult swim, and in addition to that, he didn't think Lilly would make it in one go. Spending yet another day out here would be suicide. He wanted them on the road to Bagram by nightfall.

Using his high magnification spotting scope, he scanned the length of the river, or as much of it as he could see from up here. There didn't appear to be anything out of the ordinary. There were workers in the fields, a couple of boats moored alongside the river, and a few people milling about, but nothing that aroused his suspicion.

The afternoon wore on and eventually Lilly woke up.

"Hi," he said with a tentative smile. He hoped things weren't going to get awkward between them. They hadn't laid together for long after they'd made love. Conscious of their vulnerable position, he'd pulled up his pants, grabbed his rifle and repositioned himself as lookout. Lilly had simply straightened out her clothing and with a satisfied yawn, rolled over and gone to sleep.

Now, she smiled shyly and came to sit next to him. "I must look a fright," she said, smoothing down her messy hair. It didn't help. She also had dirt stains on her trousers and a muddy mark on her blouse. Grant didn't care, she still looked beautiful to him. His heart lurched as he realized this couldn't happen again. Even though it felt right, it was wrong. Joe would have wanted him to rescue Lilly and get her safely back to England, not sleep with her on the way.

"Lilly, I think we need to talk about what happened."

She gave him a long look. "You're regretting it already, aren't you?"

He sighed. "Yes, but not because of you." Never because of her. She was amazing, but she belonged to someone else.

"Is it because of Joe?"

He nodded. "I was his best friend. We were close, closer than brothers. We went through life and death situations together and we've saved each other's lives countless times. There's a bond that develops." How could he make her understand? "I feel terrible about what happened, like I've betrayed our friendship."

She gnawed on her lower lip, but didn't respond.

"I'm sorry, Lilly, but this is wrong. As much as I wish it wasn't, I can't betray Joe's memory and his trust in me by sleeping with you."

It hurt like hell to say that, but it was the truth. There was no point in beating around the bush. He wanted to give it to her straight. That was his way.

Slowly, she sighed and gave a sad, little nod. "I understand. You're a loyal friend, Grant. Joe was lucky to have you."

He put an arm around her shoulders and gave her a squeeze. "I was lucky to have him."

They sat side-by-side and ate some of the rations as the sun began its descent in the pastel-colored sky. They were running low on supplies and had to be careful from here on out. He could catch them a fish, but didn't want to risk the time delay or the fire they'd have to make to cook it.

She told him about her mother, about how she'd died in a car crash when she was sixteen. "I hadn't even finished school at that point, so I moved in with Joe and his parents. They looked after me until Joe and I got a flat together and he joined the Regiment." She hesitated. "When I first met you, I was in a bad place."

That made sense. "I did wonder why you never socialized with us, particularly after we came back from an op. I thought it was because you didn't want to hang out with a rag-tag bunch like us." He gave her a lopsided grin, but he was only half-joking.

"Don't take this the wrong way, okay," she said, glancing down at her hands.

He nodded, wondering where this was going.

"I thought you were a bad influence on Joe." At his incredulous look, she flushed. "I know it was stupid, but I didn't know you then. All I saw was this hot, broad-shouldered guy with perfect teeth and a blonde hanging off his arm."

He nudged her playfully. "You think I'm hot?"

"Were hot," she said sweetly. "It was ten years ago."

He chuckled. "Thanks." But, then he got serious. "Actually, it was more the other way around. Joe was always the one that got a little out of hand at the pub. It was like he had all this pent-up aggression and didn't know what to do with it. I remember a few times I had to pull him out of a fight, or take him back to my place to sleep it off."

She stared at him. "I thought it was you leading him astray. To be honest, that doesn't sound like Joe."

"No, but I suppose he was always so well behaved at home. His father expected a lot of him, and then there was you..." He bit his lip, thinking he'd said too much. Joe had been a bit of a firebrand when they went out drinking. He remembered his mate saying once how perfect Lilly was, and that he couldn't be his usual carefree, foul-mouthed self around her. Personally, Grant thought she'd expected too much of him, but then what did he know? He'd never been in a long-term relationship.

"What about me?"

How could he put this in a diplomatic way? "Well, he thought the world of you, as you know, and wanted to live up to your expectations. I think he tried hard to be what you wanted him to be."

"In other words, not himself."

Grant grimaced, but gave a small nod. To his surprise, she didn't get upset, she just looked sad. "I had no idea he felt like that. I wish he'd have told me."

"Perhaps he didn't want to lose you."

"He wouldn't have lost me. We'd have worked it out."

Grant didn't reply. He'd said enough. Knowing Lilly as he did now, he reckoned they would have worked it out, if only Joe had talked to her about how he'd felt.

"We were very young when we got together," she said, after a beat. "He was my first boyfriend, the only man I'd ever been with." She glanced at Grant. "Until now." The memory of their hot and hurried love-making was still fresh in their minds. "It's hard to believe he was keeping his true self from me."

"I saw a different side to him, that's all," Grant said. "On the battlefield he was all efficiency, brave and loyal, an asset to his unit, and back home, he was just Joe, rowdy, free-spirited, always pushing the boundaries."

She shook her head. "The person you're describing sounds completely different to the Joe I knew."

"I didn't mean to upset you." He was sorry he'd brought it up. None of this needed to be said. She could have mourned him and never known how he was when he wasn't with her. It didn't matter now, anyway. Joe was gone, and he wasn't coming back.

"It's okay. I'm realizing there was so much about Joe I didn't know." She hung her head. "I wish we'd had more time."

"He was a good bloke, that's all that counts." The feelings of guilt were getting stronger. "He had my back. When I was point man and had to go into a room or a cave first, I always knew he'd be right behind me, ready to back me up. It was the same when he died. He tried to wave me away, because he knew he was in the line of fire."

Lilly gasped. "So what did you do?"

"I ignored him, of course. He'd have done the same for me." His shoulders slumped as he felt the crushing weight of that dreadful day descend. "But I wasn't quick enough. He died in my arms, right there on that mountain pass."

She welled up. "I didn't know he died in your arms. How come you never told me that?"

Grant felt the energy leak out of him like he'd been hit by a bullet. The memory was so clear, probably because he'd replayed it so many times in his head, and he realized there was no bandage for this. It was a raw, gaping wound that wouldn't heal.

"I was helping him off the pass when he took a round in the chest. It was meant for both of us, but by some miracle I didn't get hit. I held him as he died, and that's when he asked me to tell you that he loved you." He glanced at her and thought how beautiful she looked in the hazy pink light. "You were his last thought."

Tears spilled out of her eyes and rolled down her cheeks. "I'm sorry, I didn't know. Poor Joe." She hung her head. "It's such a tragedy."

That's why they could never be together.

They sat in silence, united by grief, watching the sun sink behind a purple mountain peak on the opposite side of the valley.

## 19

L illy couldn't believe how wrong she'd been about everything. The more she thought about it, the more she realized Grant was right. Joe had been extremely well-behaved at home, always polite and attentive like he was playing a part. He never let his hair down, not with her, anyway. When they went out it was usually with her friends, which meant he had to maintain his perfect boyfriend facade. It was only with his SAS mates, his true friends, that he'd allowed himself to let loose.

How had she not seen that?

She realized her preconceived notion about Grant forcing him to join the Regiment, Grant leading him astray was all rubbish. The real Joe probably wanted to escape his preordained, orderly life. He'd have craved the excitement of the SAS, the camaraderie of the close knit unit, and the ability to be himself. She shook her head as she traipsed along the barely discernible mountain path behind Grant. She'd been so blind.

But it was too late now, that was the awful thing. Joe was dead so she couldn't tell him how sorry she was. They'd been little more than kids when they'd got together, and with her moving in with him, Joe hadn't had a chance to go wild and have fun. He'd stepped up and done the right thing, taking her on and looking after her, but had he actually been happy?

The path became much steeper and Grant took her hand. He helped her over the loose stones and gravel, and steadied her when she inevitably stumbled. Her heart twisted painfully in her chest. Grant didn't want to be with her, he couldn't, there was too much guilt. The problem was, his loyalty to Joe only made her respect him more.

They were above the vegetation now in sparse, rocky terrain. If she looked down she could see for miles across the dark, still valley. The river shimmered like silver tinsel in the twilight but she wasn't fooled, nor was she looking forward to crossing it again.

Once they reached more stable ground, Grant let go of her hand. She was disappointed. She liked holding it, liked the closeness that it provided.

He'd changed since they'd left the cave. He was more wary, more vigilant all of a sudden, like he expected the enemy to appear around every corner.

"Is something wrong?" she whispered.

"I don't know," he said, which made her even more concerned. "I think we need to be careful. If anything happens, hit the ground or run for cover."

"You're scaring me." She moved closer to him.

They walked on and she tried to cast the fearful thoughts from her mind and remain positive. There was nothing to worry about. The mountain was deserted. There wasn't a person in sight. Besides, she had Grant with her, a trained SAS soldier. He'd protect her.

She pictured Grant on patrol with his unit – Joe, Rick,

Chris and Vance. What a formidable force they must have been. All fit, tough, lethal men, capable of destroying the enemy, taking out key targets, rescuing hostages and evading capture. Watching Grant stride confidently over the barren landscape, weapon at the ready, on less sleep or food than she'd had, she was filled with admiration. This was one of the most difficult and dangerous jobs in the world and he did it with such composure and self-confidence.

"Joe never used to talk about the ops," she told him, after they'd been walking a while. "He said he wasn't allowed to."

"No, we aren't supposed to. It's all confidential stuff, sometimes even unsanctioned and off-the-books."

"I've often wondered what it was like for him," she said slowly. "Is there anything you can tell me?"

Grant thought for a moment. "I can tell you about one of our missions last year, if you really want to hear about it, although I have to warn you, it's not pretty." He flashed her a look. "There's killing involved."

"I'd still like to hear."

Anything to take her mind off their current situation, and the dull ache in her heart.

He began his story, keeping his voice low and his gaze focused on the darkness up ahead. "A couple of NATO soldiers had been kidnapped in the Democratic Republic of Congo and were being held by a rebel group. We were mobilized to get them out. This was a sanctioned op. Our troop was air-lifted in, while another troop tabbed into the rebel compound on foot. It's mostly jungle out there, which is like operating in a sauna with temperatures close to a hundred degrees and a hundred percent humidity. Add to that, all the creepy-crawlies that can't wait to get hold of you and the vegetation with thorns as long as knife blades and you have some idea of what we were up against."

She listened intently, hanging on to his every word. "Was Joe in the helicopter with you?"

"Yeah. We dropped into the jungle outside the compound and advanced until we were right on top of them. The other troop had already done a seven-hour recce, so we knew where the soldiers were being held and what our POA was."

They rounded a corner, walking side by side, but apart from helping her over crumbly bits, he didn't touch her. His body was alert and even though he was telling a story, he was still looking from side to side, preempting any danger.

"Once we got close enough to open fire, it all kicked off. Rebels were running at us kamikaze-style, guns blazing, but with very little accuracy. I think half of them were high on booze and drugs. We advanced, neutralized as many of them as possible, grabbed the soldiers and got the hell out of there as fast as we could. The chopper met us at the rendezvous point and we all clambered on board." He grinned at her. "I have to admit, I was relieved to get onto that bird and out of there in one-piece."

"And you enjoy this sort of thing?" She thought they were all mad to risk their lives like this on a daily basis.

"Of course, otherwise we wouldn't do it. It is a massive adrenaline rush, but at the same time, it's also knowing we're doing something necessary. We're saving lives. We're going in as a last resort, when there is no other option." He hesitated, then said, "But, I'm always glad when an op ends successfully and everyone gets out in one piece."

She glanced up at him. "Except that doesn't always happen, does it?"

"No, unfortunately it doesn't." He stopped walking and turned to look at her. "Joe wasn't the first friend I've lost in battle. There have been others before him, but for the most part, it's something I've managed to get over. That's the way it is. We all know that when we head off on an op, there's a chance we might not come back again."

She didn't want to think about that, didn't want to consider the possibility that they might not make it back alive.

As if he'd read her thoughts, he said, "But don't worry. I promise I won't let anything happen to you."

Or him, she didn't want anything to happen to him either.

She hoped that was a promise he was able to keep.

## 20

Something wasn't right. Grant couldn't put his finger on it, but something definitely wasn't right. It was like the air was vibrating at a different frequency or something. He grabbed Lilly off the path and pulled her back against a rock.

"What?" she whispered, alarmed.

"I don't know. Wait here."

He slunk off into the night, clambering over rocks and around bushes, looking for signs of activity. It wasn't long before he found what he was looking for. Up ahead was a large encampment of insurgents. He estimated about twenty men in total. All armed. It was a search party and they were having a briefing. As he watched, they scattered and spread out into the surrounding hills. Obviously, there were too many to take on by himself, he'd be out-gunned in seconds. It was an ambush.

The goat herder.

It had to be. How else had they known they were here on this side of the valley? The only positive thing was that the Taliban had underestimated their travel time, which meant

Grant had discovered them before any damage was done. If he hadn't come scouting, they would have walked blindly into the nest of vipers. He had to get back to warn Lilly.

He backtracked to where he'd left her, making sure to keep off the contour path they'd been traversing. It was an obvious route. He found her, white as a ghost and terrified out of her wits.

"Oh, thank God," she whispered, when she saw him. She touched his cheek as if to reassure herself he was back.

"We have to get out of here," he whispered, putting a hand over hers. "They're planning an ambush up ahead."

He wished he'd taken out that herder when he'd had the chance. Now they had to improvise. And fast.

"Ambushed by whom, the Taliban?"

"Who else? Come on, let's go. Follow me and keep low. Try to make as little noise as possible."

She nodded, her eyes wide with fear.

They clambered up the hill, using clumps of vegetation and small bushes as footholds, trying not to slip and slide on the unstable ground. Anyone nearby would have no trouble hearing them, but he was counting on the fact that the enemy were at least a kilometer up ahead, still assuming their positions for the ambush.

They reached another contour path and Grant took it, backtracking in the direction from which they'd come. After another kilometer, he changed direction again, going uphill, further into the mountains. The air was becoming colder the higher they climbed.

"Where are we going?" Lilly asked, out of breath after about forty-five minutes of fast hiking.

"Plan C," said Grant. He had his night-vision scope on and so far, he couldn't see any human activity, which was good.

"Which is...?"

"I've got a friend who lives in one of the villages on the other side of this range of hills. I thought we'd pop in and say hi."

Lilly looked at him like he was mad. "A friend? Who?"

"One of my unit, Vance. He went AWOL after our last op. I think he's living in a village about thirty kilometers east of where we are now."

"You think?"

"Yeah, unfortunately I don't know for sure. That's why I didn't mention it before, but now we've had to change plans, it's worth a shot."

She gave him a dubious look. "What makes you think he's there?"

"He met a girl on a fact-finding mission to the village a few months before our last op. I was with him, actually. So were Joe and Chris. We went in as a four-man team. I knew he was soft on her, so my guess is that he came back here."

"That's all you've got to go on? A girl he was soft on?"

It was tenuous, he agreed, and thirty Ks would be tough, but it was the best lead he had, and right now, they were fast running out of options.

He shrugged. "Well, at the very least I've been to this village before so the elder will remember me. If Vance isn't there, maybe he'll help us."

She didn't look convinced. "How long will it take?"

"If we push hard, we should make it by daybreak." The village was in the opposite direction to the highway to Bagram, but the diversion was necessary. It would confuse the men searching for them.

The terrain got rockier the higher they climbed. Eventually, they located a path that ran around the peak and dipped down into a valley on the other side. The moon seemed to have disappeared altogether now, and the sprinkling of stars didn't offer much in the way of light.

Grant had had his head torch on during their descent, but now they'd come to a halt, he switched it off. Immediately, darkness engulfed them like an enormous blanket. They sat down beside a small bush and leaned back against their bergens, not bothering to take them off.

"Are you okay?" he asked, when Lilly hadn't said anything for a while.

"I'm sorry," she choked out.

"What for?"

"The ambush. It's my fault, isn't it? That goat herder gave us away, like you said he would."

Grant didn't reply. It was important she keep her spirits up. Besides, she was a civilian, she didn't look at the world from his perspective. She thought she was doing a good thing by not killing that man, and maybe she'd been right to stop him. The man had lived, thanks to her. The only problem was, now their lives were in danger.

"How did you know?" she whispered into the darkness.

"I'm not sure," he admitted. "Just a gut feeling that he'd seen us, or sensed we were there. Maybe the goats told him. I don't know."

She spluttered. "The goats?"

"Yeah, they can sense strangers."

"I should have let you kill him," she said. "Then we'd still be safe."

"You weren't to know," he said kindly. "Besides, there's no point beating yourself up about it. What's done is done, and we have to improvise, okay? I'll still get you back but it'll take a little longer."

Lilly nodded, and took a deep breath. "I will never question you again, I promise."

He grinned. "Promise?"

He heard her give a little snort.

If they wanted to make it to the village before sunrise, they had to get a move on. "You ready...?"

In reply, she lifted an arm so he could pull her to her feet. That way she didn't have to take the bergen off.

He wiped a strand of hair from her face. "It's going to be okay."

She attempted a smile. "I know."

They set off, downhill this time, which was a lot easier on the legs. The only danger was falling forwards as the path was quite gravelly, with loose stones making it difficult to get a grip.

After twenty-minutes, Grant led her off the path and down through some shrubbery. The valley on this side was higher above sea-level than the other side, and while there was no river, and the vegetation wasn't nearly as lush, it still provided more ground-cover than up at the peak. They pushed on, making good time, and Grant was glad to see Lilly seemed to have rallied a bit. She had a look of determination on her face now, that he knew only came when you'd hit your endurance level and pushed beyond that. He was immensely proud of her and he felt a surge of affection, but then he quashed it. He didn't want to focus on his feelings for Lilly, not when their relationship wasn't going anywhere.

The night wore on as they walked through the sparse hills towards the village where he hoped, or rather prayed, Vance lived.

They couldn't stroll into town unannounced, so he'd have to find his mate some other way. Not only would walking in scare the locals but it would put Vance in a precarious position, and he didn't want his mate to be compromised in his new home. He figured the villagers must be quite accepting to adopt Vance into their midst, even if he had converted to Islam. He was still a westerner and worse, a soldier, so an enemy in many of their eyes. It couldn't have been easy to integrate.

"Are you sure he's here?" asked Lilly fretfully, as they came to a stop outside a small rural community. It was more of a hamlet than a village, with about a dozen brick houses scattered about in no apparent pattern. There was a dry, threadbare field for livestock and, most importantly, a dirt road leading away from the village into the darkness.

Talking Heads' *Road to Nowhere* popped unbidden into Grant's mind.

"No, but I'm hoping. I've been here before. These people aren't affiliated to the Taliban, but they won't speak out against them either for fear of reprisals. The elder seemed like a decent man."

"So what do we do now?" asked Lilly. "We can't go around knocking on doors."

Grant gave a secretive grin. "I'll go scout about. You stay here."

He could see she was scared to be alone in the pitch blackness. "Here, you can take my headlight, but only use it if you have to. I don't want to attract any attention."

She took it, but didn't switch it on. "Okay, but please don't be long."

"I'll try my best."

He left his pack with her and, taking only his weapon and his knife attached to his survival belt, he headed towards the darkened dwellings. He had no idea which, if any, was Vance's but he knew if he was there, Vance would recognize their unit's callsign and come to him.

He slipped behind the first house, a single story stone rectangle with a small patio out front and whistled. The sound was designed to sound like a bird indigenous to the region, although there was only an hour to go until first light, so there was a possibility Vance might think it really was a tweeting bird.

At the seventh house he got lucky. He heard movement and then a door creaked. He stood behind the dwelling, upright and in full sight. He didn't want Vance to be in any doubt as to who he was.

The next moment, he felt a hand cover his mouth and the cold steel of a blade at the base of his neck.

21

---

"W hat the fuck?" Grant turned and saw Vance's grinning face behind him. "You nearly gave me a heart attack."

"I thought I was dreaming." Vance released Grant and sheathed his knife. It took a moment for Grant's pulse to return to normal. Trust Vance to pull that one on him. "Great to see you, mate."

The two men hugged.

"I see you haven't lost any of your skills," Grant said wryly.

Vance laughed, his teeth white against the darkness. "What the hell are you doing here? And more importantly, how did you find me?"

"I remembered that girl you were soft on in the village," said Grant. "It didn't take a genius to figure you'd come back here."

"I only hope the rest of 'em didn't figure that out, else my days here could be numbered."

"No chance."

It was great to see Vance again. He looked well. Thinner

than Grant remembered, and he'd lost most of his bulk, but then he wasn't pumping weights anymore. There would be time to catch up later, right now, he got straight to the point. "Listen, I need your help, mate. I've got a hostage with me, and the Taliban are up our ass. I need to get her to Bagram. Can you help?"

"Christ, you don't ask much, do you? I thought you'd quit the Regiment?"

"I have, this is a personal mission."

Vance frowned.

"For Joe. It's his girlfriend who got kidnapped. I don't know if you ever met Lilly. She's a hot-shot software designer working for GCHQ."

Vance nodded slowly. "I think I remember her. Dark hair, glasses, pretty smile. Where is she now? Back there?" Vance knew Grant would have left her in the hills while he came down to scout out the landscape.

"Yeah, we need a place to lie low, and then safe passage out of here. Do you have a phone we can use?"

"Nah, mate. No cell reception out here and not a sat phone in sight. I do have a car we can use, though. Why don't you get Joe's missus and come inside? We can talk there."

Grant nodded. "Thanks, man. I appreciate it."


TWENTY MINUTES LATER, he and Lilly sat on a richly embroidered Afghan rug in Vance's living room. There was no western furniture, however the edges of the room were decorated with cushions of all sizes and colors, and elaborate tapestries hung over the windows to keep out the cold. Two gas lamps burned in opposite corners since there was no electricity, and the house was still warm from a fire in the grate that had burned down during the night. The ex-SAS medic had made them some sandwiches and tea, which were positioned on a tray in the middle.

Vance's wife was aware that they had guests, but stayed in the bedroom. Vance thought it best she didn't meet them, and so couldn't describe them if she were asked.

"So you're Joe's missus," said Vance, giving Lilly the once-over. "I think we did meet once or twice at the barracks."

"Yes, we did." Lilly, embarrassed, cast a glance at Grant.

"I'm sorry for your loss. Joe was a good man and a good soldier."

Lilly nodded. "Thank you."

"So, how's married life treating you?" asked Grant, changing the subject. He felt uncomfortable with Vance calling her Joe's missus, even though it was true.

Vance chuckled. "It's good. We live simply, but I'm happy here. Soraya's amazing, I wish that you could meet her, and the people are warm and accepting, and they like having someone with my skills around."

Lilly frowned. "A soldier?"

"A doctor, I was trained by the NHS before I joined the Regiment."

Lilly studied him with interest.

Grant chirped, "Vance was actually trained to heal people, but then decided to join the Regiment so he could kill them instead."

Vance wasn't offended. "One of life's little ironies."

"Anyway," said Grant. "I'm glad it's worked out for you. I was worried when you disappeared."

Vance shrugged. "Adapt and overcome, isn't that what they taught us?"

At that moment a woman about Lilly's age walked into

the room, barefoot, but wearing a flowing robe and a teal scarf covering her head. It was obvious by the small bump of her belly that she was newly pregnant.

Vance immediately went to her side. "Soraya, love, I told you not to come down."

"I know," she said, putting her arm around her husband. She was very beautiful, with smooth, olive skin and eyes the color of her headscarf. She turned to greet them. "But it's not often we have guests, particularly friends of yours. I wanted to meet them."

With a roll of his eyes, Vance introduced them.

"I'm so pleased you could join us." Grant smiled at her. Soraya was lovely, with the right amount of curiosity and feistiness to keep her husband on his toes. She was exactly what Vance needed in his life. "I hope we haven't put you out."

"Of course not," she smiled warmly. "I've always been curious about Vance's past, and of course he's told me all about his friends in the SAS."

Grant raised a wary eyebrow and Vance chuckled. "Soraya knows everything about me including the Regiment, but it goes no further. The rest of the tribe thinks I'm an army doctor."

"Which you are," confirmed Soraya smiling up at her husband. It was clear she was besotted with him.

He winked at her. "Amongst other things."

Grant could see they were very much in love and he was pleased for his friend. He cast a glance at Lilly only to find she was watching him with a wistful expression on her face. He smiled, then looked away, breaking the spell. He didn't want to give her a false impression. They had to put a lid on their feelings.

Soraya noticed too, because she glanced from Lilly to

Grant and then back again, before smiling and taking a seat on the rug opposite them.

"So, what can we do to help?" she said, getting straight to the point.

"We don't want to cause you in any trouble," Grant said. "But we need to get Lilly out of the region ASAP."

"You mentioned the Taliban were up your ass," said Vance. "Could you be more specific? Like how long have we got?"

Grant smiled at how he'd automatically referred to them as a unit. Old habits died hard.

Lilly glanced nervously at Soraya.

"None of the people here like the Taliban," Vance said, putting her mind at rest. "We try not to get involved in the troubles."

"We have no poppies, you see," Soraya explained mostly for Lilly's benefit. "So there is little to bring them to our village."

"We narrowly avoided walking into an ambush about fifty klicks over the mountain." Grant nodded in the general direction of the hills. "They'll be looking for us, for certain. They know we were there. It won't take long for them to figure out which way we came."

Lilly hung her head and Grant knew she was thinking about the goat herder. Without thinking, he reached over and squeezed her hand. "It's not your fault."

She gave him a tremulous smile.

Vance noticed the touch and shot Grant an inquisitive look, which he ignored.

Soraya just smiled at Lilly. "Why don't I show you where the bathroom is, and you can get cleaned up while we let the men talk. I'm sure they've got some planning to do."

She was very intuitive. Grant smiled his thanks as she guided Lilly out the room.

"You've done well for yourself," said Grant.

"What is going on, mate?" Vance came right out with it. "Is there something going on between you and Joe's missus?"

"No, of course not," blurted out Grant, knowing that his friend would see right through him. During their time together in the unit, they'd never lied because they had to trust each other implicitly. He felt bad doing it now. "We're just friends. It's because of Joe that I'm here."

Luckily, Vance didn't push it, but Grant could tell he wasn't convinced.

"Why does she think it's her fault," he asked.

Grant told him what had happened and Vance shook his head. "That's a tough call, mate. I'd have probably done the same thing. Remember those Iraqi kids back in 2011. We let them go too, nearly cost us our lives."

Grant nodded. That had been a close shave. The kids had run straight to the Iraqi soldiers and minutes later they had a full-on firefight on their hands. Rick had taken a bullet in the shoulder, and they only just managed to get the upper hand, defeat the Iraqi soldiers, and get to the emergency rendezvous point on time.

"Did you know Joe was suffering from PTSD?" Grant asked.

Vance looked shifty. "I thought something was up, now that you mention it, but I figured if it was bad enough, he'd get help."

Grant shook his head. "Well, he didn't. Lilly said he was having nightmares, bad ones." He left out the part about Joe strangling her.

"I had no idea. He kept that under wraps, didn't he?"

They talked about Lilly, and how she'd come to be captured. Vance was interested in her work on the military software system. "That sounds excellent," he said, respect in his voice. "It at least gives the Afghans a fighting chance. The Taliban wreak havoc on these rural communities. I've seen it happen, I've helped pick up the pieces."

"You mentioned a vehicle?" said Grant.

"Yeah, I've got an old Land Rover, ex-US army, as luck would have it, bought it at a sale in Kabul last month. I can drive you back to the base, if you want?"

"You sure?" He knew Vance had gone AWOL to get away from the violence. The last thing he wanted to do was drag him back into it.

"Yeah, of course I'm sure." He grinned. "Not much excitement around here."

"Yes, but with Soraya pregnant... I don't want to put you in the shit. You don't have to do this."

"I want to, for Joe."

Grant nodded. It was how he'd felt too.

## 22

"**A**re you sure?" Lilly asked Soraya as she held up a traditional Afghani burqa. It was a two-piece ensemble made from a high quality synthetic black material.

"You're going to need something that won't attract attention," Soraya said, placing it on the bed, which was little more than a double-mattress on the floor. There was a thick rug beneath it, and colorful scatter cushions all over it. Like downstairs, an oil lamp glimmered in the corner on a low table which contained a mirror and an assortment of female beauty products.

"I believe you're very much in demand, so the more inconspicuous we can make you, the better."

Lilly smiled at her. She already wore a simple skirt and blouse that Soraya had given her after her shower. It seemed the small hamlet was hooked up to an efficient water system, probably fed by a dam or reservoir close by. "Thank you for helping me, I can't tell you what a relief it is to be clean again."

Soraya laughed which made her eyes light up. She really

was an incredibly beautiful woman. "I'm sure. How long have you been travelling?"

"I was captured three days ago on my way to the airport." She frowned at the memory. "And we've been on the run ever since."

"Poor you." Soraya sat down on the bed and studied her. "But I'm sure Grant has been taking good care of you, no?"

Lilly wasn't sure what she meant. "Er... Yes, he's been very attentive, although I have to say he sets a grueling pace. I wasn't sure I was going to make it here by sunrise."

"And he's very handsome," she added with a mischievous smile.

"I suppose he is." Lilly didn't meet her eye.

"I think he cares for you. I can see it when he looks at you."

Lilly glanced up. "Do you think so?"

She nodded. "Of course, now tell me, how do you feel about him?"

Lilly blushed.

"I'm sorry," Soraya said, "My English is not the best, so I tend to be quite direct. I hope you don't mind?"

"Your English is excellent," said Lilly, and she meant it.

"I went to the International School in Kabul. My father, thought it would do me good to learn English. I think he was hoping I'd go to university and become a doctor."

She glanced down at her belly. "That didn't happen, but at least I married one, so he's happy now." She laughed and Lilly found herself warming to her even more.

"So you are in love with him then?" asked Soraya.

"Goodness, no," Lilly stammered. "I've only known him for three days."

"Really? I am surprised. You look like you've known each other for much longer."

"Well, actually, I did meet him ten years ago, but I didn't like him very much then. He was a friend of my boyfriend, Joe."

"The SAS man who died?"

Lilly bit her lip. "Yes. It was when they first joined the Regiment. I thought he was cocky, self-assured, and one of the most arrogant men I'd ever met."

Soraya laughed. "But you were mistaken?"

Lilly frowned. "I'm not sure. I haven't worked it all out yet. I think perhaps I was mistaken, yes."

Soraya patted her hand. "I understand. He created a strong impression on you, yes?"

Lilly nodded. That he had. For good or for bad, she hadn't been able to get him out of her mind for weeks.

Soraya shrugged. "The past is the past, we cannot change it. It's the present that's important. You still have control over that. You can decide what happens next with you and this handsome, arrogant man."

Lilly shook her head. "Unfortunately, there can be no future for us. Joe was his best friend, you see. He won't betray his friend's memory." Not again.

"That's a shame," Soraya said. "You two look good together."

Lilly massaged her forehead. "I don't know. Maybe I'm confused. He makes me feel so safe, but I think I could be mistaking that for attraction."

"Having a man capable of protecting you is very attractive," said Soraya knowingly. "That's what attracted me to Vance when he first came to my village. He was here asking questions about the Taliban and he seemed so powerful and macho, but not aggressive like the other soldiers I'd met. He was kind. I could see it in his face."

"Grant said that's how you two met." They seemed such an odd match, but also so perfect for each other.

"Yes, my father was ill and Vance treated him with an antibiotic. I thanked him by cooking him and his friends dinner. After that, I knew he was the man for me."

"Really, wow. So was it when he came back here that you fell in love?"

Soraya's face clouded over. "Vance was in a bad way when he came back. He'd seen his friends killed by the Taliban and he'd left his unit. He needed a break, some time to recover from what he'd seen, and he didn't want anyone to know where he was. My father, who is a very important man in the village, took him in. Shortly after that, Vance converted to Islam, and we fell in love. At first my father was against our union," her eyes softened, "but he came around."

"I'm glad it worked out for you," Lilly said wistfully.

"Maybe it will work out for you and your SAS man too," Soraya said, getting to her feet.

Lilly crossed her fingers. "I hope so."

Soraya gave one of her enigmatic smiles. "Things have a funny way of working out. Well, I'll leave you to get dressed. Come downstairs when you're ready."

LILLY LOOKED in Soraya's mirror and did a double-take. The burqa changed her appearance so vividly she looked like a different person. But then, she supposed, that was the idea. With a small twinge of vanity, she wondered what Grant would think. Oh well, she'd find out soon enough. Soraya had told her she could use any of her make-up items so she'd moisturized her face, then lined her eyes with kohl like she'd seen the Afghan woman at work do. It helped complete the disguise. Anyone who'd known her before would have a hard time recognizing her now.

When she was ready, she went downstairs.

The men stared in astonishment when she walked into the living room. She almost giggled at the look on their faces. Soraya stood up proudly and put an arm around her new friend. "Doesn't she look the part?"

"No one will recognize you like that," admitted Vance, nodding in approval. "Good job, love."

"It's perfect," agreed Grant.

Lilly watched his face to gauge his expression, but he turned back to Vance, distracted. "I'll hide in the back, and if all goes tits up, you can say Lilly's with you and I'm a random soldier you picked up hitchhiking."

Vance leaned back in his chair. "You're taking a calculated risk, you know that, mate?"

Grant glanced at Lilly. "It's worth it to get her safe."

Vance nodded slowly.

"But, won't they be on the lookout for Lilly?" asked Soraya, casting a worried glance at her husband. "The river checkpoint is Taliban controlled."

"They'll be on the lookout for a western woman, not a Muslim woman in a burqa. Do you have a veil for her to cover her face?"

"Of course." Soraya went to get it.

"They won't risk embarrassing you by asking you to show your face," said Vance.

Lilly hoped he was right.

Grant said very little as they loaded up the Land Rover and got ready to depart. There was something worrying him, and it made her uneasy, but she didn't have time to ask him about it.

Soraya kissed Vance goodbye and whispered in his ear.

He squeezed her hand and promised to be home soon. Lilly thought it was amazing how understanding Soraya was, especially since she was pregnant and her husband was diving headfirst into God only knew what.

"Thanks for letting him help us," she said sincerely when she hugged her new friend goodbye.

"It's an important cause," Soraya replied. "We have to get you out of Afghanistan and make sure your system is safe."

Lilly felt herself welling up. "I'm sure he'll be fine," she said, seeing the concern in Soraya's gaze as she watched her husband climb into the car. "He is ex-SAS, after all."

"Inshallah," Soraya whispered. "God willing."

## 23

Grant couldn't stop casting furtive glances at Lilly from the backseat. She looked so different. The kohl made her eyes seem enormous and greener than ever, like the lush fields beside the river they'd crossed yesterday. Her alabaster skin and full, quivering lips made her appear sexy and vulnerable at the same time. He was torn between wanting to protect her and kiss her senseless.

He sighed, and leaned back against the seat. All he knew was he had to get her out of here, one way or another. His first two plans had failed, so now it was up to Vance. He had no illusions about what lay ahead at the river checkpoint. Their plan was risky. He knew it, and Vance knew it. The only consolation was it gave Lilly the biggest chance of escape, and that was his priority. Nothing else mattered.

"The checkpoint is ten Ks south," Vance called, as he took the bumpy dirt road out of the village. The Land Rover kicked up a cloud of dust behind them.

Grant focused on the operation ahead. He was well aware of how vulnerable he was. Still in his combat gear, there was no mistaking he was a soldier. Once out of Taliban territory, it shouldn't pose a problem, but until then, he was the enemy, a threat to be neutralized. Unfortunately, though, he wasn't prepared to abandon his gear for the sake of a disguise that probably wouldn't work anyway. He didn't have the dark, bearded looks of the Afghan men, and his physique practically screamed military. So if they were stopped and searched, he'd much rather be ready for it, than not.

The Land Rover had a wide backseat with a glass partition between him at the back and Vance and Lilly who were sitting next to each other up front. The partition was open so they could talk freely, but when they got closer to the checkpoint, Vance closed it so the guards wouldn't suspect they had a passenger hiding in the back.

Lilly pulled up her face veil and glanced nervously back at Grant. He gave her an encouraging smile. She was terrified. He could see it in her eyes, which was why neither he nor Vance had told her how high the risks were. She'd never have agreed.

Having evaded the Taliban for so long, they were now heading directly for them. It seemed counter-intuitive, but it was the quickest way to get her back to the base, and given her disguise, Grant thought it had a high chance of success.

He hunkered down in the back, his bergen stashed in the footwell, and pulled a blanket over himself, making sure his rifle was pointing in the right direction. The plan was for them to try to get through the checkpoint unnoticed, but if not and Grant was discovered, they could claim they'd picked him up a few kilometers back and offered him a lift.

The traffic backed up as they approached the bridge. Vance, who was dressed in his usual Afghan attire, would quite easily be accepted as a local villager. The Land Rover posed a small problem since it was a renowned army vehicle, but since Vance spoke Pashto with a local dialect, thanks to Soraya's coaching and his chameleon-like linguistic abilities, Grant didn't think his mate was in any real danger. He knew Vance had an AK-47 hidden down beside the handbrake and a combat knife under his robes.

You can take the man out of the SAS, he thought wryly.

"We're about a mile out," Vance said for his benefit, because he couldn't see anything with his head under the blanket. "I can see eight guards spread out along the checkpoint, and two more have gone into the hut."

Grant cursed silently. Ten armed men were too many to take out should there be a problem. They'd all be killed in the ensuing gunfight, along with a bunch of innocent civilians.

He knew Vance had come to the same conclusion. "I'll cover you if needs be, mate." His voice was somber.

Grant knew one thing with certainty, that Vance would have his back no matter what the situation. He'd follow him to the death, if necessary, like he would do if the situation was reversed. That was the SAS way. They worked in small units and trusted each other implicitly. You always knew you could count on each other in a tight spot. But right now, that was something Grant wanted to avoid.

"We have contact," Vance said five minutes later. "Guard approaching driver's window."

Grant waited with bated breath. He heard a tap on the window and Vance rolled it down. There was an exchange of words but it was all in Pashto, and Grant had no idea what they were saying. Then, the guard said something about the woman and Grant knew they were going to have a problem. He forced his breathing to slow down so that he was calm and controlled. He needed a clear head when the shit hit the fan.

There was a tap on the passenger window. "Leave it," barked Vance. "And keep your eyes down."

The guard tapped again, harder this time, then barked an order.

Vance replied, but his voice was measured, deliberate. Grant recognized it from the many times they'd gone into combat situations together.

This was going to kick off.

He slowly removed the blanket from his head and angled himself so he was lying on his back on the back seat, his weapon pointed upwards and towards the side window.

The guard tried the door handle and Grant heard Vance mutter, "He's clocked her."

Vance leaned across Lilly, putting his hand on his weapon as he did so, and shouted at the guard. It was something along the lines of: What are you doing? My wife and I want to go shopping in Kabul. That had been their cover story.

The guard kept trying the door, but Vance wouldn't open it.

Then he banged on it with the butt of his rifle, and there was no mistaking his meaning. He wanted Lilly to get out. Well, that was never going to happen.

The guard moved to the rear door to try and open that one. Grant was seconds away from being discovered. He exhaled, and as soon as the guard spotted him, he pulled the trigger.

Lilly screamed as the glass exploded behind her head and the Taliban guard reeled backwards, his face a bloody mess.

"Get her out of here," Grant yelled to Vance, who had jumped out of the vehicle before the guard had even hit the ground. "I'll distract them."

The other guards sprinted towards them screaming, their guns raised.

"Get the fuck out of here," said Vance, reaching for his weapon. "I'll cover you."

"No, leave it," barked Grant. He wasn't going to create a bloodbath. And before Vance had time to answer, he walked into the middle of the dusty road and put his hands up.

## 24

"What's he doing?" Lilly stared in horror as Grant walked into the middle of the road. Within seconds he was surrounded by security personnel, AK-47s pointed at his head.

She opened the car door and made to go after him, but Vance pulled her roughly back.

"Close the door," he hissed.

The checkpoint guards snatched his weapon from him, patted him down, then pushed him face-down into the dirt. One of the men had his foot on his head. They pulled his hands behind his back and handcuffed them.

"They'll kill him," she cried, as two men grabbed him roughly by the arms, pulled him to his feet, and frog-marched him off.

"I should have known he'd do that," fumed Vance, bashing his hand against the steering wheel.

"You mean he planned this?" Lilly asked incredulously. "But why? Why would he give himself up like that?"

"To save your life." Vance's voice was low. "And mine. That

guard knew who you were. If Grant had made a run for it, he would have been shot down in seconds, and so would I because I'd have been covering him. Then there'd be no one to get you to safety. The bastard knew this was the only option."

Lilly looked up to find their Land Rover surrounded by angry-looking guards, rifles drawn. Her head was still spinning after what had happened.

"Oh, God."

"Let me handle this."

Vance got out of the car, his hands also up in the surrender position.

Lilly swallowed. Somehow, it had all gone horribly wrong. Had Grant known this was going to happen? Had he planned it all along? Was that why he'd been so distracted on the drive here?

She couldn't even see him anymore. They'd taken him off in the direction of the hut. He'd killed one of their soldiers, so they wouldn't be lenient with him. Joe had told her what could happen when special forces soldiers got caught, and a million terrifying thoughts flew into her head. She fought hard not to cry, for that would blow their cover. Grant was a soldier they'd offered a lift to. Nothing more. She couldn't be seen to be crying over his capture.

Vance was busy gesticulating back up the road in the direction they'd come and she knew he was acting out their cover story. One of the guards peered in the passenger window at her, but she kept her eyes down like Vance had told her, and prayed that he wouldn't recognize her like the other man had. After a heart-stopping few minutes, the guards gestured for Vance to get back into the car and waved them on their way. Lilly felt weak with relief. They'd bought it.

"What's going to happen to Grant?" she demanded, as soon as Vance climbed back into the car.

His mouth was set in a grim line. "Nothing good, but he's a survivor. If anyone can get out of a tricky situation, it's him." He looked across at her. "Let's get you to Bagram and on that plane."

"I don't want to leave without Grant," she said stubbornly. "We have to go and get him. They'll kill him if we don't."

Vance was silent for a moment, then he said, "Listen, Lilly. I appreciate you have feelings for Grant, but he did this so you could get away. I can't put you in danger by going to rescue him now. He wouldn't want that."

It was then that Lilly started to cry. She couldn't help it. The thought that Grant had sacrificed himself for her was completely overwhelming. He'd willingly given up his life for hers.

"Who does that?" she sobbed. "Who gives up their life for a hostage they barely know."

"An SAS soldier," said Vance simply. "He's just doing his job."

"But they'll kill him." She turned her tear-stained face up to Vance, not caring that the veil had fallen away. "He killed one of their men."

Vance sighed, the inevitability of the situation evident in his furrowed brow. "He's trained to withstand interrogation so it will take them a while to find out exactly who he is. Once they figure out why he's here, they'll quiz him about you. Then they'll realize you were in the car with him and the hunt will be back on. We've got to get you out of here ASAP. Once you're safe, I can go back for Grant."

Lilly shook her head. "It'll be too late. You know it will." She covered her face with her hands. "I can't bear to think of

what they'll do to him. Joe used to tell me horror stories."
She pictured Grant stripped naked and beaten until he was
semi-conscious, his glorious body hunched over, eyelids
swollen, blood seeping from multiple wounds, and she felt
like being sick.

Vance didn't reply, he was concentrating on the road.
With the checkpoint behind them, they crossed the bridge,
the river flowing strongly below. They drove on for about a
mile until they reached a small roadside convenience store.
Vance was about to drive past, but then jerked the wheel to
the left and pulled in.

"What are you doing?" Lilly asked.

He pulled over and nodded up ahead where a reinforced
off-road vehicle was approaching at a rate of knots. It sped
by, oblivious to all in its way. Other motorists skid off the
road to let it pass. "That's for Grant," he said, his voice hard.
"They're going to take him somewhere to interrogate him."

A couple emerged from the store. The woman carried a
bag of fruit and the man two bottles of water. Vance
observed them for a moment, then he turned to Lilly. "I've
got an idea. Wait here."

Lilly watched as he greeted the couple and then had a
quiet word with them. The man looked weary until Vance
took a wad of bills out of his pocket and offered them to the
woman. She nudged her husband and he nodded, albeit
reluctantly, and took the money. Then they both looked over
to Lilly sitting in the car.

She knew what Vance was doing.

"You're going after Grant, aren't you?" she said, getting
out of the car. For the first time since he'd been captured,
she felt a glimmer of hope. If anyone could rescue him, it
would be Vance.

He frowned. "I have to get him before they move him to

a secure location,'" he said. "I'm sorry, Lilly, but these people will take you to Kabul. From there you can call the Afghan police and they'll make sure you get safely back to England. It's probably better this way, anyway. If they figure out who you are, they'll be looking for the Land Rover."

Lilly nodded. She was okay with that.

She gave Vance a big hug. "Thank you," she whispered through her tears. "Thank you so much."

"Good luck, Lilly," he told her. "And for what it's worth, I think Joe would have been happy to see you two end up together."

"What do you mean?" She felt the heat stealing into her cheeks.

He winked at her. "You know exactly what I mean. Now off you go. I'll send your man back to you as soon as I can. I promise."

GRANT WAS STRIPPED NAKED, his wrists secured in front of him with plastic ties. He was in a concrete room, about twenty by twenty, with the door behind him and two windows on the wall in front. The blinds were broken causing thin shards of light to refract across the floor. He was on his knees, the butt of a gun pressed against the back of his head.

"Who are you?" shouted the man standing behind him.

Grant didn't react. He felt a blow to his ribs, then another, and he fell over onto his side. Another pair of arms picked him up and pulled him back onto his knees. He hadn't even realized there was another man in the room. On the way here in the van, he'd been given a right working over. His left eye was swollen shut and his nose was filled with clots. He had a mild concussion, and was pretty sure they'd dislocated his collarbone when they'd dragged him out of the transport vehicle and shoved him in here. The room stank of blood and urine, and he didn't want to guess what else.

"Who are you?" the man shouted again. Grant caught a whiff of stale coffee and cigarettes. The nakedness and yelling was supposed to unsettle him, but he'd gone through worse on selection. He'd been here before, and that gave him some comfort. This wasn't a new experience for him.

Grant let his head drop and tried to appear as subdued and as feeble as he could. It would give them the effect they wanted. If he'd gone all gung-ho and said fuck you, they'd only have beaten him up again. So he played into their hands.

"You are US army," sneered the other man, spitting on the floor.

Grant looked contrite, like he'd been found out. The less they knew about him the better. Once they realized he was British SAS, they'd put two and two together and know he'd been part of the hostage rescue. It didn't matter that he was no longer in the unit.

So far, his capture hadn't reached the Taliban leaders up in the mountains who were presumably still searching for them, but it would soon. And when that happened, all bets were off.

When he didn't answer, he got a rifle butt in the head. The shock sent him reeling over onto his side again. He didn't move, waiting for the pain to subside and hoping they'd think he'd been knocked out. They kicked him in the back to make sure, so he moaned incoherently, but didn't move. Hopefully, they'd think he was too far gone to continue with the interrogation. They weren't giving it their all, anyway. It was a half-arsed attempt to discover his identity. From what he'd seen so far, this lot were not particularly organized and there was no clear chain of command. These were all things that acted in his favor.

Grant dozed off, curled up in the fetal position on the cold, concrete floor. There was nothing else he could do right now. When his head cleared a bit, he'd take stock of his surroundings and try to figure out how the hell to get out of here before the Taliban insurgents came for him. While he was still alive, he had a fighting chance.

When he opened his eyes, or rather his one eye that wasn't swollen shut, he felt marginally better. His head wasn't throbbing like a freight train anymore. That was a good sign. He sat up, and using the wall for support, staggered to his feet. His legs felt a bit wobbly, but that was probably due to the concussion. He made his way to the closest window and peered out through the blinds, into a yard of some sort. With a surprise, he realized he wasn't in a secure compound, but in a house and he was looking out onto a back garden. As he watched, an armed man walked by, presumably on guard. Grant stretched his neck, ignoring the explosion of pain in his shoulder, but couldn't see anyone else. He knew there must be more than one person guarding him until the others came back and carried on with the interrogation.

If he was going to get out of here, now would be a good time. The house was relatively insecure, there were no bars on the windows and the door wasn't reinforced.

Luckily his hands were tied in front of him, which made maneuvering easier. He tried the door handle, but as expected, it was locked. There was nothing in the room except a wooden chair and a small puddle of fresh blood which belonged to him. He went back to the window. The guard was nowhere to be seen. Grant waited, counting the seconds until he appeared again. In total, the guard had been gone for almost five minutes. As soon as he disappeared the second time, Grant moved the blind aside and made a fist. He punched a small square out of the bottom window. It made a soft pop, but he doubted it was loud enough to hear. The soft dirt outside masked the sound of falling glass. Without wasting any time, he used the shards that remained in the pane to cut through the plastic ties.

While he was doing so, he assessed the situation. Two options: Bash down the door or go out through the window. Either way was risky. Breaking all that glass would draw the guard, but the breaking door would draw whoever was still in the house. He went with the window. At least that was less of an unknown.

The chair went flying through the window, closely followed by Grant, who'd used the blind to protect himself against the ragged edge. Despite this, he still got cuts on his hands and legs. As expected, he heard the sound of running footsteps, but made it to the corner of the house in time to send the guard flying as he emerged around the corner. He bent down to pick up the fallen AK-47, but before he could get a shot off, he heard a voice shout, "Put down the weapon!"

Slowly, he turned to see two guards standing in the doorway, pointing their semi-automatics at him.

*Fuck.*

He considered taking them both out, but knew the odds were against him. On the other hand, surrendering would mean getting hauled back inside and given another beating, and this time they wouldn't be so lenient.

He hesitated, feeling strangely detached like he was in someone else's body. The two men watched him warily, waiting to see what he'd do. Their instructions were to guard him, not kill him. He might have information that was useful or he could be ransomed.

What these guys didn't know was the Taliban rebel leaders wouldn't be thinking along the same lines. That decided it for him. He wasn't going to give them the satisfaction.

He was going to go for it.

## 25

As Grant put his finger on the trigger, he heard a voice yell, "Get down!" Without thinking, he threw himself face first into the ground. A volley of shots from behind drilled into the two men, sending them flying backwards into the house.

The next minute an arm reached down and grabbed him.

Vance.

"Christ, am I glad to see you," Grant muttered, wincing as his fractured ribs complained at the ungainly lift.

"You crazy bastard, you were going to go for it, weren't you?"

Grant gave him a lopsided grin. "Always wanted to go out in a blaze of glory."

Vance shook his head. "Come on, the car's around the corner."

They legged it down the road to the Land Rover, which Vance had cleverly parked facing outwards in someone else's driveway to avoid suspicion. Shouts and automatic rifle fire could be heard charging up the road behind them.

"Let's get the fuck out of here." Vance put his foot down and screeched out of the driveway, nearly flattening two Taliban soldiers in the process. They dived out of the way just in time. The Land Rover raced down the suburban road, kicking up dust and pebbles in its wake. In the rear view mirror, Grant saw the two soldiers pick themselves up off the ground. Soon, they were joined by two others. All four raised their weapons and fired. The back window exploded, shattering glass fragments over the interior of the vehicle.

Grant ducked instinctively, but Vance merely laughed and gave them the finger.

"Thanks mate," said Grant once they'd put some distance between themselves and the house where he'd been kept. "I owe you one."

"Rubbish. You'd do the same for me."

It was true, he would. That was a given.

"Where's Lilly?" Grant knew Vance hadn't had time to drive her to the air base. His mate had done exactly what he would have done had the situation been reversed. He'd followed the security forces to the safe house and waited for the right moment to attack. While he appreciated the rescue, his priority had been for Lilly to get to safety. He hoped Vance hadn't compromised that.

"Don't worry, your girl is safe." He grinned. "I persuaded an Afghan couple to drive her to Kabul. She's probably safer with them than she would have been with us."

That was true. He knew Vance must have bribed the couple. U.S. Dollars, most like. "Appreciate it."

"I promised her I'd get you back in one piece." Vance shot a sideways glance at his mate. "You are in once piece, aren't you? It looks like they did a number on you."

"As far as I know," he said, coughing and holding his

ribcage. "They didn't go to town, thank God. I think they were waiting for the heavies to get there. Thought I was U.S. army."

"Idiots," said Vance, checking in the rearview mirror and indicating. Thanks to his advanced driving skills and counter terrorism training, he'd easily evaded the cavalcade of cars that had sped down the road after them.

He turned right onto a narrow dirt road filled with potholes. Grant winced with every bump. The searing pain in his shoulder was brutal and the throbbing in his head was back.

"Sorry, but I thought we'd better ditch the Land Rover. I know a guy who's got a motocross bike you can borrow."

"Excellent." Not that the off-road bike would do his ribs or shoulder any good, but he wasn't complaining. It was the fastest way back to Bagram and would avoid detection because he could use it on the gravelly off-road paths. It was the perfect mode of transport for this terrain.

Vance grinned. "I knew you'd approve. And, if you hurry, you might catch Lilly before she leaves."

Grant leaned his head back onto the headrest. "Now why would I want to do that? She's safe. The Afghan police will ensure she's put on a plane. Job done."

"Come on, mate. Don't give me that shite. I know how you feel about her."

Grant closed his eyes. "It doesn't matter how I feel. She's Joe's missus, remember? I did this for him."

"Bollocks. She was Joe's missus, now I reckon she's yours."

"It's wrong," murmured Grant.

"Hey, don't go to sleep, you've got a concussion." Vance elbowed him in the ribs, which made Grant gasp in agony.

"Easy," he clutched his side and exhaled.

"That's better. You've got to stay awake. When we get to Farzaad's house, I'll take a look at you. That cut on your head needs patching up."

"I'm fine," Grant said, fighting the darkness that was descending over his vision. The next minute, he passed out.

"Don't you listen to anything I say," complained Vance when Grant opened his eyes.

"Where am I?" Grant tried to sit up, but the room spun. With a groan, he lay back down again.

"You're at my friend, Farzaad's house. Don't worry, we're safe here for the time being."

It all rushed back to him, making him feel even giddier. The capture, the beating, the escape and the manic last few moments when he'd been convinced he was going to die.

"How many fingers am I holding up?" said Vance.

"Fuck off."

Vance laughed. "Okay, but take it easy. You were in a worse state than I thought."

"Christ, what have you done to my shoulder?" Grant tried to move it but couldn't feel a thing.

"I popped it back in for you, and gave you a shot to numb the pain. You've also got three fractured ribs. I didn't opt for morphine because I knew you'd want your wits about you, besides, you can't ride a bike if you're high."

"Damn straight."

"That'll last for a couple of hours, until you get to Bagram, but it's only a temporary measure. Once you're there, you'll have to go to a hospital so they can sort you out properly."

Grant got off the bed. The spinning had subsided now,

but his head felt foggy, like he'd knocked back too many shots of tequila.

"It'll take a while for the concussion to wear off. I'd give it a few hours before you take off. Farzaad is happy for us to stay here."

"How do you know this guy?" asked Grant.

"He's Soraya's sister's husband's brother, if that makes any sense."

Grant shook his head. "I'm sorry I asked."

Vance laughed. "He's a good guy. Come on, let's get some food into you. He's laid out a spread in the kitchen."

"Yes doc."

It took four hours for his head to clear, and another shot of pain-numbing medication before Grant felt able to get on the bike.

Vance stood beside him. "So, this is it, mate. Take care of yourself. I'm not always going to be around to get you out of trouble, you know."

Grant chuckled. The piss-taking never stopped.

"You too." They hugged.

Grant said, "Seriously, mate. I appreciate it. I couldn't have got Lilly out of here without your help."

"Don't mention it. Just invite me to the wedding."

Grant shook his head. "You never let up, do you?"

"That girl's in love with you, mate. If you don't go after her, you'll be doing yourself a disservice."

Grant sighed. "What about Joe?"

Vance gave him a long, hard look. "You know, I think Joe would approve."

## 26

L illy stared out of the window of the military transport aircraft that was taking her back to RAF Northolt in South Ruislip, west London. The sky was a cobalt blue above her and below, all she could see was a sea of white, fluffy clouds. About ten minutes ago, according to the Captain, they'd crossed into international air space. She was going home!

The Afghani couple had driven her all the way to Kabul and dropped her outside the central police station, so all she'd had to do was to walk in and tell them who she was. Within minutes she'd been taken to the police chief's private office and several frantic phone calls later, her identity and employment status within the Afghan government had been verified.

They, in turn, made several calls to the British Foreign Office and before she knew it, she was whisked off in an armored, air-conditioned vehicle to the nearest air base and put on a plane. It seemed the Afghan government couldn't wait to get rid of her.

Not knowing what had happened to Grant was killing

her. Was he alive? Had Vance got to him in time? Had he been badly injured by those Taliban guards? She tried to relax. Of course Vance had got to him. He was a professional special forces soldier. If anyone could do it, he could. Besides, he'd promised.

Once he'd handed her over to the couple outside the convenience store, she'd seen Vance get back into the Land Rover and knew he was waiting for the armored van carrying its prisoner to return. There was only one road across the bridge, so it had to come back that way. Presumably, he'd followed it.

Tears filled her eyes. Please let him be alive.

Exhausted from her ordeal, Lilly slept most of the way home. To her surprise, when she landed, Pat was waiting for her at the air force base. She was inordinately happy to see Joe's broad-shouldered bear of a father.

"Lilly! I'm so glad to see you. Where's Grant?" He looked around as if he expected him to get off the plane behind her.

She shook her head and burst into tears. Pat held her while she sobbed.

"What happened?" he asked when she'd pulled herself together. He feared the worst and she felt terrible for misleading him.

"I don't know where he is," she admitted. "He was captured at a Taliban checkpoint and Vance went after him. I have no idea if...if they're even alive."

"Vance?" Pat stared at her. "As in Vance from the unit?"

"Yes, he's living in Afghanistan now. We went to him for help."

"I see. Well, why don't you come home with me and you can tell me all about it."

Pat knew she had no one else, and she didn't fancy going

home to an empty flat. She smiled at him gratefully. "That would be wonderful."

DAYS PASSED without any word from Grant. Pat pulled all the strings he could, he spoke to the embassy in Kabul, the Afghan Government, even the police, but no one seemed to know anything about the ex-SAS squad leader. It was like he didn't exist.

"That's how they're trained," Pat told her. "There's no accountability, most of the time the government won't even admit they've been deployed to a region. If they get caught, they evade and escape under their own steam."

But they were beginning to fear the worst.

Lilly continued to stay with Pat. It reminded her of when her mother had passed away and they'd invited her into their home. Nothing much had changed. The furnishings were still the same, albeit a little more threadbare, the photos on the mantelpiece were exactly how she remembered. Pat hadn't changed a thing. She'd been so young then, so in need of support. She'd be eternally grateful to Pat and Val for taking her in.

Pat seemed to enjoy having her stay. She thought maybe it reminded him of Joe or like her, of how things used to be. At least she could talk to him about her experience and he understood. He hadn't been captured before, but he'd had a long career in the Paratroopers and had done many, many tours to the Middle East. They spent hours discussing the situation in the Middle East and the work the armed forces were doing out there. He didn't divulge anything about the special forces, but Lilly knew he had his finger on the pulse at Westminster.

One evening after dinner, they were sitting in the

garden together as had become their habit. Lilly was scanning the internet on her laptop, looking for any news of a captured SAS soldier, while Pat read the newspaper. He glanced at her screen and said softly, "We might never know."

"Know what?" But her heart dropped. She didn't want to acknowledge that he might not be coming back.

"We might never find out what happened to him." He put down the paper. "Sometimes, they never come home."

Lilly felt like a red-hot poker had penetrated her heart. "Don't say that," she whispered. "I know he's still out there somewhere."

Pat studied her, a knowing look in his eyes. "You care for him, don't you?"

She didn't know how to respond. Would he be upset that she'd moved on from his son? That she'd fallen in love with his best friend?

"You're barely off that laptop searching for information, you jump every time the phone rings, and you're the first one outside when a car pulls up. We're both desperate for information, but it strikes me that this goes a little deeper for you, doesn't it?"

"I don't know how it happened," she admitted, unable to meet his gaze. "But somewhere along the line I fell in love with him, and now he's gone because he sacrificed himself for me." Her voice broke. "I owe him my life."

She'd told Pat what had happened at the river checkpoint.

Pat reached over and squeezed her hand. "I miss him too, love. And I feel responsible since I was the one who sent him over there to get you."

Lilly hadn't considered that. Pat never showed his feelings. He was always just there – strong, dependable and in control. Like Grant. Another surge of longing hit her in the chest.

"I'll be forever grateful." She got up and gave him a hug.

"You're like a daughter to me, Lilly," he said gruffly, hugging her back. "I don't regret sending the team in, but I'm sorry it hasn't worked out the way we expected."

She nodded, fighting to hold back the tears.

"If it's any consolation, he's a tough bugger, and with Vance helping him, there's a good chance they made it out alive."

Lilly knew he was saying that to make her feel better, but she prayed he was right.

SHE HADN'T GOT around to telling her friends she was home. As far as they knew, she was still working abroad. The nature of her work for GCHQ meant she couldn't divulge what she did, which made close friendships difficult. It was better this way for now. Until she found out what had happened to Grant, she was in a state of limbo, unable to concentrate on anything other than scrolling for information on him.

GCHQ sent a representative to Pat's house to debrief her, and she could confidently tell them the military system had not been compromised, however, she did point out that the Taliban had got hold of her keycard somehow. It turned out they'd bribed one of the men in HR to hand it over once she'd left. They, in turn, confirmed the system was online and working well. They were reading the Taliban's movements, and the Afghan government was mobilizing troops to drive them out. There was talk of the special forces helping them out.

The representative assured her that she could come

back to work whenever she was ready, and to a promotion, but to take a few weeks off to recover.

A promotion.

It was so surreal, she told Pat one night at dinner. She'd been kidnapped, nearly blown the entire operation, and got back home to find she'd been promoted.

But her heart was heavy. It was now a week since she got back, and still no sign of Grant. Even Jamie, Cole and Alex had popped in to see if there'd been any word. They'd spoken to Pat about going back out there to find him. Pat had said he'd see what he could do and spent the next few hours on the phone, but by the sounds of things, the MOD wasn't cooperating. They had bigger problems.

Lilly had gone upstairs to cry herself to sleep. One of these days she was going to have to face the fact that Grant was gone and wouldn't be coming back.

## 27

L illy was sitting outside in the garden flicking half-heartedly through a magazine when she heard a motorbike pull up. Pat had gone out, and she was alone at the house.

She squinted into the sunlight. It was a pretty snazzy bike painted a metallic blue with a diagonal red stripe along the side. The man getting off it wore jeans and a black T-shirt, but she couldn't see who it was due to the helmet. She stood up, thinking this must be one of Joe's mates who'd popped in to see Pat. Then she recognized the physique and her heart jumped into her throat.

No, it couldn't be? Could it?

She moved closer, willing it to be true.

Please let it be him, she prayed.

Then he took off the helmet and placed it over the handlebars. She'd recognize that hair anywhere. With a yelp, she sprinted across the grass and threw herself into his arms.

He winced, then laughed and hugged her gently.

Tears streamed down her face, but she didn't care, she was so happy to see him. "I thought you were dead," she cried. "Oh, God. I thought you were dead."

"Takes more than a bunch of disorganized soldiers at a checkpoint to kill me," he said, holding her at arm's length so he could study at her. "It's so good to see you."

She gazed lovingly at his face, so handsome, but at the same time damaged. He had a black eye and a nasty wound at his temple covered with two strips of gauze. It was then she noticed he had a sling around his neck, but he wasn't wearing it.

"What happened?" she asked, as he slipped his arm back into it.

"Dislocated shoulder," he said. "But Vance popped it back in for me. I've got to wear the brace for support, but it's a bitch to drive with, so I don't."

She laughed. It was amazing to have him standing there, in Pat's garden, in the flesh. She could hardly believe it. Her hand ached to reach out and touch him, convince herself he was real. He'd shaved, gone was the beard that she'd grown used to, but he looked great this way too. He looked perfect, in fact. She couldn't take her eyes off him.

He was also gazing at her, his eyes roaming over her face, making her feel warm inside.

"I'm surprised you recognize me without all that dirt," she joked, trying to keep things casual, when all she wanted to do was throw herself into his arms and kiss him senseless.

"I did wonder," he replied, his eyes sparkling. "Especially since this is Pat's house. I thought maybe he'd met some hot babe while I'd been away."

She rolled her eyes. "Pat's been letting me stay here. After what happened, I didn't want to be alone."

They stared at each other for a long moment. Lilly felt her heart beating in her throat. Then she said, "Come inside. I want to hear all about it. How did you escape? Did Vance get you out?" She led him inside through the French doors.

"I'll tell you everything, but first I must say hi to the old guy. Is he around?"

"No, he's in London trying to convince the powers that be to let your ex-SAS buddies go back to Afghanistan to find you. He's been so worried. We all have."

Grant spread out his hands. "No need. As you can see, I'm back safe and sound."

"I'm so glad," she whispered, tears springing to her eyes. Embarrassed, she blinked them away.

"So how did you get away?" She sat down on the spacious, leather sofa in the living room. It was the same one that had been there when she'd moved in with Pat and Val over ten years ago. It was well-used and the leather had faded on the armrests, but it was big and comfy with plenty of space for two. Grant sat down beside her.

"After you left, I was taken to a safehouse somewhere in the suburbs. Luckily, they hadn't moved me to a secure compound yet. They still didn't know who I was, or what I was doing in the country. They hadn't linked me to you."

She folded her legs underneath her and listened. There was tension in his face as he talked, and she could tell the experience had left its mark.

"They interrogated me for a while, but to be honest, they weren't that enthusiastic about it. I think they were waiting for the heavies to arrive. When they left, I broke a window and got out. Vance provided some much needed backup," he grinned. "And, of course, there was a bit of a shoot-out, but we escaped without too much trouble."

Thank God he wasn't hurt. "I was so worried. I kept scouring the internet looking for information but there was nothing."

"No, I didn't tell anyone where I was going. It was safer that way. I made it to the U.S. air base on the off-road bike Vance's relative lent me, but because I wasn't there in an official capacity, they patched me up and sent me on my way. I managed to hitch a lift on a military cargo plane heading back to Northolt last night."

"Were you badly hurt?" Her eyes dropped from his face to his shoulder and then to his torso. Outwardly, he looked as fit and as strong as ever.

He shrugged. "I had a bit of a concussion and a few cracked ribs, but nothing serious."

She shook her head. "I'd hate to see what you call serious."

"I've had worse."

Lilly stared at him, this crazy, brave, insanely hot man that she'd had all to herself for four days. She loved him, she knew that beyond a doubt, but he couldn't love her back. Joe stood in the way, a constant obstacle between them. And she didn't have a clue what to do about it.

GRANT HAD NEVER FELT this nervous before, which was ridiculous considering what he'd been through in his life. The war zones, the operations behind enemy lines, the violence... but he was terrified to tell Lilly how he felt about her.

Looking at her now he was so overcome by emotion, he could hardly get the words out. Sharing his feelings wasn't his strong point. Feelings had no place in the world he lived in – used to live in. But he was out of the Regiment now, his last operation over. All he had wanted to do was to get home and see Lilly, but now that he was here, he was struggling to find the words.

"Lilly, I–" he broke off, unsure of how to continue.

She watched him, wariness etched onto her face.

"I know," she whispered. "I know there can never be anything between us. You don't have to say it."

"I wasn't going to "

"You weren't?" Her eyes lit up. She looked so hopeful he wanted to grab her right then and there and kiss the life out of her. But he had to get this out. It needed to be said.

"I'm sorry about how things ended in Afghanistan. I was so conflicted about Joe. He was my best friend, and he cared about you so much. It felt wrong doing what we did."

She didn't reply, just stared at him with huge eyes that matched the color of the grass outside.

"But when I was captured, all I could think about was getting back to you." He glanced heavenward. "I only hope Joe understands because...because I love you, Lilly." He exhaled. "Wow. I've never said that before to anyone, but I mean it. I want you in my life, and not as a friend, but as my girlfriend."

Lilly's eyes filled with tears and she launched herself at him, wrapping her arms around his neck. "Oh, Grant. You don't know how I've longed to hear you say that. I thought there was no way you'd ever let yourself be with me. I'd given up hope."

"How can it be wrong?" he muttered into her shoulder.

"It's not wrong." She disentangled herself and smiled at him. "Joe gave us a gift. It was because of him that you came to rescue me. And I know you blame yourself for his death, but if you'd died on that mountain pass too, I wouldn't be alive right now. You saved my life."

"Vance told me that the translator had been coerced. His family had been threatened, so even if I had vetted him more thoroughly, it wouldn't have made any difference." He touched her cheek. "I'm really glad I could be there for you."

There was very little talking after that. Grant kissed her hungrily, relishing in the taste and scent of her. It had been too long since he'd last held her in his arms, and he'd been dreaming about this moment since he escaped. She reciprocated with an enthusiasm that matched his own. Soon they were both breathless and sizzling with desire. "I'm going to take you upstairs now," he growled, getting off the sofa and pulling him with her. "I'd carry you, but I don't think my ribs would allow it."

She laughed and led him upstairs to her bedroom. "Pat won't be back for a while, so we can take as long as we like."

They collapsed onto the bed in a tangled mess, half-kissing and half-undressing, desperate to feel each other again. "This is so much better than a cave," Grant murmured, as he positioned himself on top of her.

Lilly giggled, and wrapped her legs around his waist. "Don't mock it. That was the best sex I've ever had."

He gave her an intense look. "I'm only just getting started."

Several hours later, they ventured downstairs to make something to eat. They'd worked up quite an appetite. Grant commandeered one of Pat's beers and poured Lilly a glass of wine while she made them sandwiches. Then they went outside to eat.

Grant felt like he was the luckiest guy in the world. He could have so easily perished out in the field with Joe, or even at the hands of the Taliban had Vance not rocked up to bail him out. And now he had this gorgeous woman by his side, who he could love and cherish for the rest of his days.

"Cheers," he said, clinking glasses with her. It didn't get much better than this.

A car pulled up as they were finishing up.

"Pat's home," said Lilly, taking the plates to the kitchen. "I'll let you say hello."

Grant strode round the house to the driveway and chuckled at the look on Pat's face as he climbed out of the car.

"Bloody hell, Grant. I've had half of Whitehall fighting over whether to sanction another op to go and get you. Do you know how much trouble you've caused me?"

Grant chuckled and gave Pat a hug. "Well, now you can tell them not to bother."

Pat thumped him on the back. "Am I glad to see you."

They walked inside.

"I told Lilly you'd make it back okay." Pat winked at Lilly who'd come out to meet them. "Didn't I, darlin'?"

She laughed and went to Grant's side. He put an arm around her waist. "You did indeed."

Pat glanced at the two of them and smiled. "You know, I'm happy to see you two together. I can't think of anyone else my Joe would have entrusted his girl to."

Lilly gave him a hug. "I'm so glad, Pat. We were worried you wouldn't approve."

Grant met Pat's eye and nodded. "You know I'll take good care of her." And he meant it with all of his being. Lilly was a gift he would never take for granted.

Pat cleared his throat. "Now let's have a real drink and you can brief me on what happened. Hereford and Whitehall will want an update, and I have a proposition for you."

Grant looked weary. "What sort of proposition? If it involves Afghanistan, I'm not interested."

"Africa, actually," said Pat. Both Grant and Lilly stared at him like he was mad.

"Grant's not well enough to go anywhere, Pat," she began. "He's got to rest and recover."

"I'm not talking about Grant," said Pat mysteriously. He opened the side cabinet and got out the whiskey, then he sat down at the dining room table. "Lilly, be a dear and grab us some glasses."

Lilly did as she was told, although she gave him a hard look. "I don't want you sending Grant away again, Pat. I mean that. I've only just got him back."

Pat winked at her. "I was thinking Cole would be perfect for this job."

"Cole?" Grant narrowed his eyes. "Pat, what have you got cooking?"

"Well, I've been spending a lot of time at the Ministry of Defense lately, and I've realized there's a need for an unofficial SAS force, a unit who can do everything the legit teams can do, but without the red tape, like rescuing hostages, providing protection for Ministers, that sort of thing. So I pitched the idea to the powers that be today, hoping the first operation would be to go and get you back. They're considering it. It would help them out of a lot of sticky situations, particularly when they need prompt action and the official channels take too long."

"You mean we'd run our own unit?" Grant felt a fluttering of excitement in his belly. He'd been wondering what the hell he was going to do with himself now that his military career was over. Lilly would go back to work, and he wanted to be useful, except he was dreading getting a proper job. Most guys in his position ended up as glorified security guards or worse. There wasn't much legal work for men who were trained killers.

"Yeah, sort of like a rogue unit," said Pat.

"Wait a minute." Lilly came back with the glasses, she'd brought the rest of the bottle of wine in for herself. "What are you saying, Pat? That Grant would be heading out on dangerous missions again?"

She glanced worriedly at Grant, and his heart surged. It felt good having someone care about him enough to worry. He'd never had that before. In the past, when he'd gone on operations, it was only his Commanding Officer who cared whether they came back or not. And not for any warm, fuzzy reason either.

"I'm asking Grant to lead it," said Pat, twisting the lid off the bottle of scotch. He turned to Grant. "I'll be the middle-man, the link with M.O.D. You can pick and choose your assignments. You can operate as a unit, or individually, depending on the requirement. It'll be protection work, some hostage extractions, destruction of communication lines, you know, the usual special forces remit."

"My kinda thing," said Grant.

Lilly rolled her eyes. "I can see you've already decided, haven't you? You want to do this?"

Grant shot her an apologetic grin. "I have to work, love, and you heard Pat, we can pick and choose our ops. As the leader, I'll mostly be involved in strategy and planning, and I promise never to set foot back in Afghanistan."

Lilly kissed him. "I'm going to hold you to that."

Pat folded his arms across his body and leaned back in his chair. "Excellent. I'll let the others know you're in."

"What others?" said Grant, after he'd thrown back a finger of scotch. It warmed him all the way through his body. It felt good to be alive.

"The others – Cole, Jamie and Alex – they can't wait to get started."

"Sounds like fun," said Grant, shaking Pat's hand.

"Oh, boy," said Lilly, and poured herself a very large glass of wine.

ROGUE UNIT

# ROGUE JUSTICE

## LOUISE ROSE-INNES

AMAZON BESTSELLING AUTHOR

# ROGUE JUSTICE
SAS ROGUE UNIT BOOK 2

**A safari turns deadly in this fraught, sensual romantic suspense by Amazon bestselling author, Louise Rose-Innes.**

Former special forces operative, Cole Armstrong isn't looking for love. Far from it. He'd much rather focus on his current assignment, protecting his target – a key witness – whilst pretending to be a tourist on an organised safari in southern Africa. Then he meets Anna, and everything changes.

Tour guide Anna has been a wanderer her entire life, then she meets the British SAS soldier who turns her world upside down. When poachers attack their party and their guide and driver ends up dead, it's Cole who leads them to safety. Except things are about to go from bad to worse – and suddenly Anna's heart isn't the only thing that needs rescuing.

*Find out to what lengths the former special forces soldier will go to claim the woman of his dreams. This is a full-length, stand-alone romantic suspense with a satisfying happily-ever-after.*

Click here to read *Rogue Justice*, the second book in the sizzling SAS Rogue Unit series.

# CHAPTER 1

"I'll be home soon. I promise."

Anna stood on the hood of their German, ex-army, overland vehicle and yelled into the phone. The reception around here was dreadful, but then they were in the middle of Namibia, on the west coast of Africa, miles away from civilization. The only thing taller than her right now were the burnt-ochre sand dunes that undulated in the distance.

"You'd better be," her brother said, the underlying bitterness evident in his voice. "I can't hold this position open forever. I pulled a lot of strings to get you this job."

"I know, and I'll be there. Just one more week, okay?"

She breathed in hot, dry ground, fragrant wildflowers, and burning wood. It was heady, intoxicating. Their campsite was fifty yards away, at the onset of the Namib desert. Any further and they'd be able to wiggle their toes in the sand.

This was Day Four of the overland tour she was leading through southern Africa. She still had to pinch herself when she thought about it. What an adventure!

They'd left the Orange River Canyon behind earlier that day and driven out into the desert to set up camp. Tomorrow, they'd rise before dawn and trek into the dunes to watch the sunrise. It would be a once-in-a-lifetime experience. She couldn't wait.

In fact, this whole trip had been amazing. Okay, strictly speaking, she shouldn't really be the tour leader – what she knew about surviving in the wild was scary – but by some lucky twist of fate, the role had fallen into her lap. Now here she was, leading this group of tourists across the most beautiful continent on the planet. It was the stuff dreams were made of.

Besides, it wasn't like they were roughing it.

They had an African navigator and a driver. She was just there to show the passports at the border crossings and book the hotels – when they weren't camping, that was. To be honest, she preferred being outdoors to the low budget hotels the tour operator favored. Why settle for a crummy African hostel when you could have this? She stared up at the vast expanse of sky, and sighed. It was bliss.

"One week, Anna, then I'm going to give it to someone else. I've got a pile of resumes on my desk and all the candidates are better qualified than you."

*Why don't you say it like it is, bro?*

It was just like him to rub it in. Felix never could resist an opportunity to make her feel like shit. He'd been doing it their whole lives. Perhaps he'd learned it from their parents.

He was the clever one. The good looking one. The one with the Stepford wife who'd given them two adorable grandchildren.

She was the failure. The drop-out. The spinster.

She gritted her teeth. "Thank you."

He sighed and hung up.

Rolling her eyes, she pocketed the phone and leaped off the hood of the truck to the dusty ground, her muscular legs and hiking boots handling the one-meter jump with ease.

The sad truth was, she needed that job.

Flitting around the world waitressing and doing bar work didn't exactly pay very well, and she wasn't getting any younger. It was time to put down some roots, buy a place of her own. And *this* job was the way to do it.

Her grandma's voice echoed in her head.

*"There will come a time in your life when you'll find what you're looking for. Then you can stop running."*

Those were the last words she'd ever said to her.

Dear grandma. Her rock. The only person who truly understood her.

A week later, she was dead. A massive stroke, the doctors said. Anna bit down on her lip. She hadn't had a chance to say goodbye.

The campfire beckoned. The sun had set, and the sky was a kaleidoscopic fusion of pinks and purples, deepening to indigo in the east.

Her tour group sat in low camping chairs around the blaze like some sort of primitive tribe, silhouetted against the bright orange glow. In the distance, she could hear drumming, but that was from a group of hippies on the other side of the encampment. Occasionally, a dog barked or there was an outbreak of raucous laughter. Someone had opened a bottle of brandy and was passing it around.

She smiled and joined them. They were a great group; friendly and chatty, all except *him*.

She glanced around. As usual, he was nowhere to be found.

"Anyone seen Cole?"

Cole Armstrong.

A strapping beast of a man with chiseled features, dirty blond hair and a gaze that stared through you and into your soul at the same time. It was unnerving.

She lowered herself into a vacant chair and stretched her long legs out in front of her. The heat from the fire was so fierce she had to shuffle back a bit. Out here in the middle of the bush, they needed the fire to keep the wild animals at bay. Even though they were at a campsite, there were no official boundaries. Animals were free to roam over the uninhabited landscape and often wandered into the camp in search of scraps. Wild dogs, jackals, and baboons were not uncommon.

"Not for a while, honey," replied Monica, an attractive redhead from Texas who was fulfilling a lifelong dream by coming on an African safari after divorcing her second husband.

"I was due a little reward after putting up with him for so long," she'd confided to Anna over welcome drinks the first night of the tour.

"What about you, Phil?"

"Nope, sorry Anna. Haven't got a clue where he went."

Phil and Cole had been late arrivals on the tour. An Australian couple had canceled at the last minute and Head Office had rung to ask her to slot them in. It had been a mad rush to rebook all the hotels and visas in their names, but she'd managed. Chaotic last-minute admin was one of her superpowers, she'd been doing it long enough for herself on her travels to far-flung parts of the globe.

At first, she thought Phil and Cole were traveling together, but that didn't appear to be the case. In fact, they couldn't be more different. Phil was middle-aged, corporate and unadventurous, while Cole was... *not*.

He was a hulk, well over six-foot – a fact she appreciated

being five nine herself – with broad shoulders and a mouth-watering physique. The well-worn denim jeans he was fond of wearing hugged his thick thighs and his khaki T-shirt was so tight it could have been spray-painted on. He was also moody, broody and mysterious.

And a distraction she didn't need.

She sighed. He was also put on this earth to irritate her.

*Where the hell had he got to now?*

This was not the first time he'd gone walkabout. The guy acted like he was on a self-drive safari, the way he carried on.

"I suppose I'd better go and find him," she muttered, getting up again. She couldn't have him wandering around the desert after dark. God only knew what could happen, and it wouldn't look good if she lost a tourist on the first week of the tour. Even if he was the most annoying one on the trip.

Ali, their African navigator, and Poko, their driver, had both turned in for the night. They didn't socialize with the group, despite Anna's best attempts to persuade them. They preferred to keep to themselves, setting up camp away from the rest of the tour.

"Want some help?" asked Anton, a lithe, sinewy South African who was on the tour with his wife, Dee. They wanted to see southern Africa before they emigrated to Canada. This tour was their swan song, and they were enjoying every glorious moment.

"No, I'll be okay. You stay and enjoy yourself."

The brandy was going down fast and everyone was in good spirits. She didn't want to spoil their fun.

Where could he have gone?

Knowing Cole, it would be somewhere off the beaten

track. He always went where he wasn't supposed to. It was like he had a death wish or something.

In the Cape Point nature reserve, he'd hiked up to the point when everyone else had taken the vernacular. In Simon's Town, he'd gone for a swim in the freezing Atlantic Ocean and had been out there so long, she thought he'd been eaten by sharks.

But that wasn't the worst of it. In Cape Town, he'd opted to *climb* up Table Mountain instead of taking the cable car and they hadn't seen him for the better part of the day. He'd waltzed into the hotel dining room in the middle of her presentation, sweaty and disheveled, yet still hot enough to make every woman in the place swoon.

With no apology, whatsoever. *Jerk.*

She admired his spirit of adventure, but the strange thing was, he didn't look like he enjoyed it. Not once had she seen him smile, and sometimes, when he thought nobody was watching, he looked downright miserable, almost like he was in pain.

The man was an enigma.

She did a lap of the campsite. The hippies were singing folk tunes and playing bongo drums, but there was no sign of Cole.

He wasn't going to make this easy for her. She ought to leave the errant bastard out here to get mauled by wild animals. It would serve him right for blatantly disregarding the rules. Not that she was a stickler for them, far from it, but there were safety measures he had to adhere to. This was Africa, after all, not Hyde Park.

His British accent was so goddamn sexy. And the way he studied her through half-slitted eyes when he thought she wasn't looking. Eyes the color of the African sky.

She gulped. He knew how to turn her into a puddle of mush.

Being tall and blonde, she often had men check her out, but not like this.

Not like *him*.

With one steamy glance, Cole transformed her into one hot mess, but at the same time, there was a hint of arrogance there, like he was waiting for her to fuck up.

Or maybe that was her insecurity talking. Her parents had been doing that her whole life, which was why she'd left home as soon as she was old enough, not even bothering to finish her degree.

Now, whenever she felt vulnerable, her first instinct was to run. To get away from the source of ridicule as fast as possible, except out here, there was nowhere to run. And she was responsible for these people, her tour group. She couldn't up and leave no matter how uncomfortable the rough-and-ready blue-eyed beast made her feel.

"Cole!" she yelled into the rapidly darkening night. "Where are you?"

Silence.

Only the distant drumbeats and the muted howl of a night predator echoed back at her.

She stomped to the edge of the campsite, to where the hard, dusty ground turned into soft sand and shone her flashlight into the darkness. It was a small, pocket-sized one and the glow didn't extend further than a few meters.

It was basically useless.

Where else could he have gone?

She glanced around, the hairs on the back of her neck stood up. It was creepy out here, alone in the dark.

There wasn't anywhere to go.

The desert stretched for miles in front of her, all the way to the coast where it was beaten into submission by the relentless waves of the Atlantic Ocean. Behind them was bushland, dry and arid, and beyond that, the town of Swakopmund, where they'd stocked up on supplies before they'd driven out here.

He'd be insane to go traipsing through the bush alone.

She checked the truck; it was empty and locked for the night. The unused equipment was safely stored inside.

Heaving a great sigh, she turned away and began to retrace her steps back to the campsite. She'd give it another few hours. Then, if he hadn't returned, she'd have to inform the authorities. Bloody-minded, self-centered Brit.

"You looking for me?"

She spun around.

"There you are! Thank God, I thought you'd gone missing."

He'd snuck up so quietly she hadn't heard a sound. It was as if he'd materialized out of the darkness.

"I told you before, I can take care of myself."

It was too dark to see his face clearly, but she knew those uncompromising eyes were locked on hers.

She swallowed. "You might have let me know you were going off on your own. I was worried."

She saw a flash of white teeth. "There's no need. I'm fine."

*Clearly.*

Was he laughing at her? Making fun of her?

Her shoulders tensed and her chin lifted a notch. "It wasn't just me. Everyone's been asking where you are. It's dangerous out here at night, you know. There are all sorts of wild animals lurking about."

"I know, I read the signpost at the entrance."

But he ignored it.

"If anything happens to you, it's my ass on the line," she huffed, losing her patience. "But I don't suppose that matters to you."

"Nothing is going to happen to me," he retorted in his deep, taunting voice.

"You'd better hope so because out here, there is nobody to come to your rescue."

He tilted his head. "Except you."

The cheek of the man. She turned on her heel. "I wouldn't count on it."

And stomped back to the campfire.

To Continue reading Rogue Justice, click here.

## SAS ROGUE UNIT SERIES

Going Rogue

Rogue Justice

Loveable Rogue

Wild Rogue

Rogue Agent

Rogue Vengeance

Rogue Hunter

Rogue Legend

Browse the series on Amazon - https://amzn.to/3euyXKT

# ABOUT THE AUTHOR

LOUISE ROSE-INNES is an Amazon bestselling romance author. She writes about brave, warm-hearted men and the strong, independent women who love them. Find out more about Louise and subscribe to her newsletter on her website – www.louiseroseinnes.com.

Printed in Great Britain
by Amazon